Rejected by Blood

By

Mazzy J. March

Rejected by Blood

A Mated in Silence Novel

Digital ISBN: 978-1-68361-85-2

Print ISBN: 978-1-68361-525-5

Published by Decadent Publishing LLC

Academy Books from Decadent Publishing You Might Enjoy

The Lycan Academy by Mazzy J. March

First Howling

Second Growl

Third Snarl

Jaded Love

The Academy of Fire and Ash by Mazzy J. March

Betrayed by Dragons

Coveted by Dragons

Mated to Dragons

Alien Academy by Jenna M. Jett

First Contact

Second Sighting

Third Encounter

Shifters of Consequence

Survivor

Legacy

Triumph

Dominion

Torn

Tether

Tremble

Tinsel

Mated in Silence

Rejected by Fate

Rejected by Blood

Rejected by Birth

The Sciathain Academy

<u>Veiled Wings</u>

Prologue

Jillian

The forest still loomed large around the little cabin. Dark pines and alders, hickories and honeylocust, and so many others I couldn't name. Magda promised to teach me, but her old joints weren't always up to a long trek anymore, and I didn't want to cause the person who'd shown me such kindness even a moment of pain. Shifters aged slower than most others, but even we had our declining years. My friend, half-shifter and half-witch I believed, although I never asked, had likely lived well over a century, maybe two. Her wisdom and mentorship had enabled me to survive when the pack sent me to live in the forest on my own.

Just a young teen, I had been fostered by various members who, while they were not cruel, had never seemed especially invested in my life. And when the previous alpha announced that I would be living on my own, I had been completely unprepared.

My home had been barely fit for anyone to live in, at the time, and even with Magda's help, I hadn't made it much better. Inside, it was clean, at least, and organized. Funny how easy it is to organize when you have almost nothing. And it smelled good inside because of all the herbs hanging from the rafters. I crafted teas and remedies, with Magda's assistance, and hoped one day to be able to help others as she did. Some of the pack had begun to come to me for various culinary herbs and things.

As lonely as I was, their brief calls were like my social life.

Before Dean, I thought I'd accepted my lot, grateful for what scraps came my way, even though I didn't know why I was singled out to be alone...or why I had no voice.

But Dean makes me feel like I have a voice even without the ability to talk. He makes me feel...whole.

Which is why my interest, my wolf's interest, in two new shifters to the pack is so confusing.

Chapter One

Jillian

So far, I'd avoided the other two men my wolf demanded I run toward for the last few weeks. Dean was enough. He was more than enough.

"Where are you going, mate of mine?" His voice popped my ever-present overthinking bubble and plucked me back into reality. I'd just finished a longer shift than usual, since harvest season was over and the winter preparations were in full swing. Winters around here were harsh. Despite the alpha barking about more supplies and more firewood for the entire pack, it never seemed to be enough. Inevitably, as the snow began to melt, you would hear axes chopping at trees that simply wanted to finish their winter rest.

Good thing I didn't rely on the pack's provisions to get me through. I'd never depended on them and never would. Not that they would allow it anyway.

But this year was a little different. This year, I had more than just me to keep warm and fed.

Didn't feel like a burden one single bit.

I held up my basket as an answer. This time of

year boasted mushrooms and green onions that grew wild in the forest, but the pack wasn't aware of the fact, or else they just didn't care. Season by season, the forest gifted different herbs and sprigs of flavorings.

"Okay. Be careful. I have this to finish and then I'm coming home." Dean walked over to me after putting his axe down and grabbed me by the hips, pulling them against his as he kissed me until I was downright delirious.

When I was a little girl, I'd always wanted an affectionate mate. But as I grew up and became more and more pushed away from everyone in the pack, I gave up hope that he would actually appear. Learned to be grateful for the scraps tossed my way, the occasional kind word from someone who didn't pay enough attention to be rude to me. And Magda. I was always grateful for the half-witch who lived even deeper in the forest than I did. But a mate? I'd decided that would never happen.

Until Dean. His hugs and kisses, long winter nights of lovemaking, and casual but loving compliments. Sometimes I even forgot about my unfortunate affliction.

Fate seemed to like me after all, just a little.

I left after making sure my knees were still

working and found myself hopping over roots and winding around tree trunks in my search for treasures for that night's soup. Dean never complained about having basically the same thing every night. He'd gotten into the pack's good graces, thanks to his hard work and perseverance, despite being mated to the outcast. So several times a week, he now came home with a fresh loaf of bread and once, some cinnamon rolls. Bread made my soup taste like, well, more than soup.

"You should be more careful walking out here alone...Callista."

I rolled my eyes. I'd never seen this man before, but he must've been drunk or something. My name wasn't Callista, not even close.

I shook my head and turned slightly, pointing toward the pack common area. He was probably lost and inebriated. It happened more than one would think around here.

"No, I'm not here for them. I'm here for you. You look so much like your mother. It's incredible." He moved with his hand extended as though he might touch me, but I slapped it away. I grimaced at the mushrooms I had just spotted but would have to forget since this jerk was blocking my path and apparently was a touchy-feely sort. My basket swung as I walked away, but the man followed me.

Whirling on him, I intended to give him the stink eye of the century but probably failed. He did look like I'd slapped him.

"You don't even know who you are?" He stepped toward me but I stood my ground. My wolf snarled and snapped at another male so close. "Can you speak?"

My wolf took over then. She wasn't putting up with this any longer and forced the shift.

Bad people. Won't find us again. Need mate.

Chapter Two

Could life never let me have a moment of peace?

I raced through the forest, zigzagging right and left to try to keep the guy who had accosted me and called me *Callista* from following. I wasn't sure if he was a wolf or not, having been in too much of a hurry to get away from him to take the time to assess. He did know about the pack compound, obviously, but might be one of those who thought it was a rural settlement or something.

No. I leaped the stream halfway home, already swelling with runoff from the low mountains where our caves, the ones Crystal Canyon got its name from, were located. No, he was a wolf. His scent just made its way into my brain and confirmed the fact. But all that told me was he could catch up to me and could use his nose to do it. With that in mind, I doubled down my speed and gave up on the zigzagging. If he chose to follow me, he'd get there eventually.

Arriving at home, I shifted on the porch and leapt inside, slamming the door closed behind me and letting the bar drop over it. When Dean moved in, I had very little way to secure the space, but he'd added this old-fashioned but effective feature. And right now, I couldn't have been happier to have it.

He turned from where he was adding some vegetables into the pot on the wood-burning stove. He'd bought that, too. I used to have to cook over the fire in the hearth. Still did, sometimes, but for most situations, the stove sure was helpful. "What's wrong?" He hustled over and wrapped his arms around me, bringing my naked body into contact with his flannel shirt and jeans. Comforting, warm, wood-smoke scented...and everything I needed to feel better.

His lips rested on the top of my head. Waiting patiently for me to respond, but not in words because I had no words. Hadn't as long as I could remember, although I wasn't 100 percent sure I hadn't been able to talk as a small child.

Way back in my mind, it seemed I could remember words coming out of me, but I wasn't sure if it truly was my speech or just a desire for it to have been true. I communicated with nods and headshakes and as I got a little older, with marginally literate notes. Never feeling like I got across what I was trying to or barely able to. For so many years I'd wanted more...

But Dean never made me feel like less. From almost the first moment, he made me feel like more. He not only took the time to "listen," in a way that was hard to define but nobody else ever had, he taught me to read and write in a mature way. Honestly, although I knew my lack of education had contributed, on some level I'd always worried that I might not have the ability to achieve more. That maybe everyone but me knew that.

His arms were my salvation, but when I tried to move back, in search of my pad or whiteboard, so I could tell him what happened, he just started talking. He told me all about his day, and after he released me long enough to get something to wear, he filled my bowl with his concoction and kept talking.

It was odd. Usually he was the best listener. But if I wanted someone to listen to me, I needed to be a listener myself. I was no longer freaked out by the man in the forest. It wasn't the first time I'd been approached, nor would it be the last. I knew that on some level. He hadn't offered me violence, and I'd been home long enough to believe he hadn't followed me.

I didn't know why not, but for tonight, locked in our cabin, I could turn my attention to my mate and try to forget everything else. I'd been good at sectioning off my life for a long time. Having a pack who treated me as if I was not really one of them could be so painful...but the forest with its beauty and bounty brought me joy. Now there was the part of me who loved being with Dean. Then, of course my wolf.

Were there parts of me I'd forgotten somehow? It was already crowded in my head. I suddenly became aware that Dean was studying me from across the table. So much for being a good listener. I knew he'd been talking about his day, about working and something about the betas arguing. But not why any of that was relevant to us. I waved a hand in apology, but he just shook his head and stood, took my hand, and led me to our bed.

This was such a strange night. Not that he wanted to make love to me. We did that just about every night and many mornings as well. Had we not been having such a totally odd evening, I would have been surprised if he hadn't been trailing kisses down my neck. But even under these circumstances, I couldn't resist the heat of his lips and his caresses. Didn't want to. His love was the best part of my life, and as he stripped me of my clothes, murmuring sweet, sexy things, I set everything else aside.

After all, I was good at putting things in boxes in my mind. And this box, or section or part, was the one that told me life was worth living. So I wrapped my arms around his neck and kissed him back. Responded to his touch. Welcomed him into my body while my heart rate increased and my breathing grew shallow, panting. When his thrusts sped up, and he ordered me to come, I did just as he asked. Fell over the edge of the world into star-speckled darkness. He never came before me, never left me unsatisfied. His heat poured into me, then, and I held on tight.

But when he fell to the side and spooned me, I wished more than ever in my life that I was more. That I could speak soft words into the night, ask him why today of all days he wasn't listening to what I needed to tell him. Why he talked all evening about seemingly random everyday things when I needed to share something.

I wasn't about to get my white board, though, and light a lantern, not now. Now was the time for drifting off to sleep and leaving questions for tomorrow.

But when I awoke, it didn't seem so important. The man in the woods obviously had mistaken me for someone else, and Dean had just had a busy, frustrating day at work. It happened to everyone sometime. He was just so good, I expected perfection. And he was still human.

Chapter Three

Another couple of weeks passed, and the work on our "rural commune," as many in the local town called us, was amping up. We raised most of our own food, and sold the surplus at the local farmer's market and at our own highway stand in summertime, and we shared the profits, so they weren't completely wrong.

Previously, my "share" had been almost nonexistent, but with Dean in the picture, we benefited more. Everything about this man improved my life. And I loved him so much, my heartbeat sped up every time he came into the house or my line of sight anywhere. To even consider more was greedy in the worst way, and judging by his reactions to those in the pack with more than one mate, it was so beyond his world view, he'd never understand.

And someone like me finding one mate? Was a miracle and one like Dean? The biggest miracle ever.

After days of working in the communal gardens and fields, I found a day to visit the forest and do my real job. Gathering herbs both medicinal and culinary as well as other useful plants was what I enjoyed doing best. When you're all alone in the forest, it doesn't matter if you can speak. I was 100 percent relaxed there. Maybe a little bit too at ease.

A while back, I'd been returning from Magda, my half-witch mentor's home when I'd overheard two men speaking on their way through the forest. I'd hidden and listened to their deep rumbling voices. Usually I was uncomfortable with strangers. Even more than with other pack members. Thus, my hiding. And usually my wolf was equally unhappy about someone she didn't know approaching us. But she had reacted differently to the pair. Ears perked up, sniffing the air, interested.

I had heard they had basically just wandered into the compound and made themselves at home. Somehow. And I'd seen them around from time to time but hadn't exchanged a word with them. Which was better. So much better! If I lost Dean, I'd be back where I was before. No. Worse. Because before, I hadn't fallen in love.

Fiddlehead ferns were a big favorite at this time of year, and I had two baskets with me in hopes of filling them for a planned feast. One Dean had made me promise to attend. I was very nervous, since I hadn't been to any big gathering since moving out into the woods. So...none as an adult at all.

My perhaps unwise ease in my surroundings, combined with my focus on the task at hand and thoughts of the party to come allowed, made me careless. At least that's my excuse. But when the loud crunch of a footstep behind me sounded, I jumped so high, my fiddleheads tumbled onto the ground.

"Did I startle you?"

The voice, deep, rough silk, stroked over me, and I choked on my own spit in outrage at not being able to reply. I almost hadn't brought a pad and pen because nobody ever came to this part of the woods. To his credit, Shane, as he introduced himself after pounding on my back until I could breathe again, didn't laugh.

Finally I bent over and found my writing implements among the spilled ferns. *Nobody ever comes here. Yes. I was startled.* My writing had improved greatly since Dean's lessons began.

"Really? I think it's one of the nicest parts of the wood. Feels so ancient with the big trees and plants I haven't found anywhere else. Isn't that why you're here?"

I snorted. *I am collecting fiddleheads for the feast.* I wanted to write that unlike some people, I didn't have a lot of time for aimlessly cavorting among the ancient giants. Only for collecting their bounty. But that was a lot of scribbling.

"And I come along and not only surprise you but make you drop them. Let me help!" He dropped to his knees, landing on a goodly portion of the ferns, and I suppressed a groan. Enthusiastically, he piled them in the baskets before I could stop him. Now I'd have to sort the intact from the crushed before the bad started rotting all over the good. "There, that's all of them, isn't it?" He looked up at me from his position, a hopeful smile lifting the corners of his lips.

I nodded.

"Then maybe you'll walk with me a bit? Then I'll escort you home." As if it were a done deal, he tucked my baskets under one arm and used the other to link with mine. "It's nice to have company."

With the way he held me, I couldn't write, and therefore couldn't protest, I needed to sort the ferns, to get more ferns...and I needed not to be so close to a man who had my wolf excited and not in a negative way.

She was all wound up and rumbling inside me.

"You are Jillian, right?" He chatted on about the trees and the birds, the other ferns...all the things that made this part of the forest so special. Sometimes I half expected a dinosaur to appear from behind a tree. Maybe a saber-toothed tiger. My fantasies knew no bounds but this was one that could not happen. Any thoughts of him stopping and taking me in his arms, of his kissing me and telling me he was my mate must be suppressed.

Dean did not deserve to be thrown off guard that way. He'd mentioned more than once his lack of understanding on the nontraditional relationships in the pack. And I couldn't really explain that they were actually very traditional. Just because humans didn't often choose to have several partners didn't mean we had to be the same. My wolf was very enthusiastic about adding to our family, but Dean...

How would that pay him back for everything he'd done for me?

I waited for him to loosen his grip then stepped away and scribbled on my pad. *Nice to meet you but I have to go home.*

"Absolutely, I'll walk you there."

I shook my head. I need to get more ferns first.

"Well I can't just leave you here all alone," he protested, a lock of hair falling over his eyes in his distress. "I can wait."

Nobody ever comes here...I'm safe.

"I came here, so obviously some people do…" Could this guy not take a hint.

Thank you but please go. I thrust the page at him then turned and double-timed it through the forest. Another minute, and my wolf would have had me kissing him. I couldn't fight her forever.

Chapter Four

Dean

"We have a summons from the alpha, Jillian. He says first thing this morning." I loved her name, the way it felt right on my tongue, so I said it as much as possible.

My mate had come in from picking ferns with something on her shoulders the night before—I could just tell. Her eyebrows remained dipped down and her posture was tense. She seemed distracted.

I wished she could tell me with her own voice what was wrong.

And I wished I could fix whatever it was for her.

She turned toward me and rolled her eyes. Meetings with the alpha were not her favorite thing, and that was a nice way to put it.

"I know you don't want to go, but I don't want you to get into trouble."

Shrugging one shoulder, she got out of bed. She wasn't shy anymore. Just a few weeks ago, she would have hurried to cover herself up, often taking the bedsheet with her, but now she had no qualms about walking around me in nothing.

I wasn't complaining, not one bit.

"I was also thinking about going to town to call my parents. Did you want to come with me?" I'd never broached the subject of my parents or my family with her. She'd brought it up several times, but since I was still wrestling with it myself, I didn't see the point.

She whirled around and then jumped into bed with me. Concern was written all over her face.

"It's okay. I'm sure they are worried. I just want to tell them I'm okay and not to be concerned. I'd like to introduce you to them one day, but I know it will be a while. I'm not really ready to face them yet."

Her shoulders slumped before she reached for her whiteboard.

Am I keeping you from them?

Of course she thought it was her fault. It tended to be her thing.

"No, of course not. I'm still coming to terms with this turning into a hairy wolf thing, so I sure as hell am not ready to walk into my parents' house like nothing is happening. I won't ever tell them, but that's going to be hard. When I do go see them, I want you to come."

She nodded once and then did the sweetest thing. She touched her chest, right over her heart and then reached out to put her hand over my heart. It was Jillian's way of saying she loved me. My wolf knew it. I knew it.

"I love you, too, but we should get to the alpha before we're in trouble."

We got dressed in a bit of a hurry before walking hand in hand toward the compound.

"Don't you two have work to do?" Jerad barked out as we passed him.

"We have a summons from the alpha," I clipped back, tired of his shit. The man was on a constant power trip, and it made him look like a jerk.

"Oh, okay. Well, get to work as soon as you're finished."

At the alpha's house, we waited outside while we were announced. As I stood there, a thousand ruminations went through my head. Were we in trouble? If we were, I would take Jillian from here. It wasn't the first time I'd entertained the idea, but it was the first time I'd actually planned in my head on where to bring her and how to provide for her needs.

She shook our connection, our tangled hands, plucking me from my catastrophizing and back into the present.

I winked at her, trying to let her know I was okay,

and she blushed. Not blushed like I'd said something cute, but the deep-red hue in her cheeks said she was way more than flattered, she was turned on.

And damn it all, if that didn't turn me on as well.

"Dean, Jillian, please come in." The alpha himself had opened the door to his office. That alone should've tipped me off that something was up. Usually a beta or someone else would let us in.

"Jillian and Dean, I'm assuming you know this person? Although, Jillian, he seems to think your name is Callista."

I knew that man. He was one of the ones whom I had encountered in the woods, asking all kinds of prodding questions about my mate, where she lived, and if I had allowed it, I assumed he would've asked many, many more.

Jillian's heart thrummed at a rabbit's pace in her chest. My wolf felt the tension and panic tornado inside her, making him on edge and ready to defend her, protect her from whoever in the hell this man thought he was.

The man bowed at the waist and looked down.

"There's no need to bow to me," the alpha said, going back to his desk to sit in his chair. The thing creaked as he leaned back.

"Forgive me, alpha, but my bow was not for you. My bow was for her—Callista."

Chapter Five

Jillian

I reeled back, only Dean's grip on my hand keeping me from landing on the floor. *What the hell?* After a couple of deep breaths, I freed my hand and grabbed my whiteboard and marker from the bag I carried everywhere. Since I'd begun drawing, I had my pastels and drawing pad in there as well. But those did me no good now.

The alpha leaned a hip on the front corner of his desk and arched a brow. Clearly he waited for me to respond.

I am Jillian. I lifted the whiteboard so they could all see.

Dean had more to say. "Who is this guy? He accosted me in the forest asking, some very personal questions, and now he claims my mate is this...this Callista? Alpha, Jillian is under your protection, and lately our lands have been overrun with strangers who seem determined to disturb our peaceful existence."

He nodded. "What do you ask of me, Dean? Would you have us erect walls around our property?

Surely you know it's not feasible. The cost alone would be prohibitive, much less the labor needed to raise our food. No one else seems to be having these issues."

"No, of course not, alpha. I know that's not the answer, even if there was all the money in the world. But my mate is getting very upset at being accosted so often, and I wonder if maybe there's another solution? I know I am new to this life, but I understood pack land was sacrosanct. Sure, humans might wander in by accident, but other shifters like this...this guy should know better. Unless you gave permission for his entry?"

Oh. Dean shouldn't be confronting the alpha this way, especially in front of an outsider. I expected something bad to happen. He was the absolute leader of our pack and nobody should be telling him how to do his job or demanding to know why he might have made a decision, or even what it was if it didn't affect them personally.

Although this did affect us...

I swallowed and turned the board toward myself again. I wiped it clean with the little cloth then considered what to write. I had never made a demand upon the alpha, never requested anything more than a little food, the occasional garment... For the most part,

I took care of myself before Dean came to help. After I was sent to my cabin at least. I was an orphan who relied upon the goodness of the pack members. They had raised me, even though I was not a child of any of them, nor a grandchild or any blood relative as far as I'd been able to determine. In fact, now that I thought of it, I hadn't asked questions about my parents since I was very small.

Maybe after we got Dean reconnected with his, I could pursue that further. Or maybe what happened to them was so horrible, everyone was shielding me? Was I strong enough to face the truth?

"Jillian? Did you have something else to say?" The alpha's glare was directed at me, something nobody wanted to happen to them. "Did you want to speak with this man?"

I shook my head emphatically. Even if I had the full power of speech, I would not. Something about being called by a different name set off so many red flags or maybe flares? My peace of mind was in danger, and I already had something else doing that. Why couldn't I have a normal life? Get up, eat, work, make love, maybe shift and run through the woods and hunt some stuff. Shifter normal.

"I did not grant this wolf permission to set foot

upon our lands." The alpha stood up and pressed the button on his desk, summoning a beta. Jerad, who had no doubt followed us here and probably had his ear pressed to the door, opened it way too fast.

"Alpha?"

"Escort this stranger to the border of pack lands. I don't expect to see him back here again." Dismissing the matter from his attention, he rounded his desk and sat down.

But the outsider was not quite ready to be dismissed. "Alpha, this isn't over. I am not sure why her highness is denying her identity, but I will return with proof. Please ensure that Cal...that Jillian remains here. I will return with proof of her identity." He turned and moved out the door, followed by Jerad.

The alpha bent over a stack of papers on his desk as if my whole world hadn't been set on its ear. What did he mean, her highness?

"Alpha, what does this man want? Why did he say that about my mate?" Bless Dean for having the words I did not.

"Who knows why people do what they do. You may leave."

I stumbled out of the alpha's house onto the porch and stopped there, my mind circling around those words. Her highness? Denying who she is? I'd been with this pack since I could remember, since I was very tiny at least. If any of what he was saying held truth, wouldn't it have come to light long since?

Ridiculous.

"Let's go home, Jillian. The man was clearly out of his mind. Maybe this Callista whoever she is left him for some other wolf or something. We needn't let it ruin our day."

I nodded, but I couldn't let it go. He might be out of his head, or there might be something to it. If he returned, I'd talk to him. Fear couldn't rule my life forever. But it wouldn't be in the alpha's presence. He hadn't been nearly weirded out enough by what the stranger said.

Chapter Six

Jillian

We didn't let the strange man in the alpha's office ruin our day. Well, on the surface we didn't.

There was a palpable tension between us, though Dean tried to squash it with kisses and sweetness. He was talented in that department.

"What should we read tonight?" he said, pulling me from my thoughts and back into the present. I knew that tone from my mate. He was baiting me, and I fell for it every time. "I got this today. It's one of my favorites and very romantic. What do you think?"

I plucked the book from his hands after wiping my fingers on a cloth napkin that used to be a dish towel.

The first word was pride. I knew that much. But the second, I pointed to and shrugged. Shrugging was the best nonverbal way to ask Dean a question. That and a cocked eyebrow.

"Prejudice. *Pride and Prejudice.* It's pretty long, but I really think you will like it."

I flicked through the pages and immediately knew he would have to pause almost at every sentence and explain a word. Still, I couldn't tell him no. His green eyes shone brightly, and his smile melted me in place. No way I would disappoint him. He was so damned cute when he was like this.

Nodding, I pointed back to my bowl. Though the stew was cooked over the fire again, against my mate's protests, it was foreign to me. Dean called it chili and had torn through two bowls full.

I didn't really care for it, but food was food. I wasn't picky, not by a long shot.

We had a secluded spot in the forest where a small layering of rocks made a waterfall and, for us, a shower. It was on the edge of the pack's lands and I knew no one would ever come there. At least I hoped. Some of the places I'd sworn that about were now filled with traffic it seemed. But I wasn't going to give up the magic of skinny-dipping with Dean. Voyeurs beware. Interrupted shifters tended to grow fangs.

"I never knew simple could be this amazing," he whispered in my ear. I had my legs wrapped around his torso, while my arms were rounding his neck. My face must've given me away again because he chuckled, jostling us both as the water swirled around us. It had been cold at first, and we both gasped as our dry bodies hit the cold water, but after a while, our shifter temperatures kicked in and the chilly pool was refreshing—comfortable even.

My breasts were pressed against his chest and, when we were close like this, his heartbeat soothed me, drumming with mine.

"I'm not complaining, mate. I thought life had to be complicated. College, work, running around like crazy, and then you die. This...life with you is incredible. I wouldn't have it any other way."

Once he stopped talking, his mouth moved to my neck where he sucked and kissed the tender skin right below my earlobe. My back arched, and I yearned for more. My core pulsed with need as my back hit the edge of the pool.

I wished I could tell him to take me right there.

Good thing I didn't have to. My mate always seemed to read my mind when it came to sex.

"Let your legs go a little. I've got us, Jillian."

I loosened my legs as his hands roamed down, grabbing my ass, cupping and kneading the muscles there. "Oh, sweetheart, you have no idea how much I want you right now."

Hell yes, I did. Probably half as much as I wanted him.

Our lips met while my fingers tangled in his hair,

right at the nape. Dean's hair was softest there, and I sought it every time he was near.

"You're so ready for me, Jillian. Always ready for me." He pushed himself inside me, and I fisted his hair tighter as my hips rocked of their own accord. He whirled us around, his back against the rocks. He bent his knees a little and shifted me onto his lap, in the water. The pressure on my core was new like this and, in mere seconds, my world shattered around me. Dean cried out my name just three pulses later.

We were left in a wet, shallow-breathed heap, our foreheads pressed against each other while we came down from the mountain.

"Let's get you home. My wolf is pretty pissed I have you out in the cold."

He whisked us both onto the shore, and we dressed quickly before heading back to the cabin hand in hand, both smiling like we'd just had our first time again.

Well, my first time.

The cabin was warm. I heard the familiar snaps and cracks of the fire as he stirred up the coals to a blaze.

"Just a few pages tonight. You've worn me out."

I opened my mouth to a wide O, and he laughed

loudly.

We didn't make even one page before coming together, this time on the bed. He positioned me on top again, giving me sweet instructions while he touched me everywhere, all the time asking me if I liked certain things.

I shattered on top of him and we fell asleep like that, my body plastered to his. Wrapped up in his arms, I was in complete bliss.

"Jillian,"' Dean whispered sometime later. The sun wasn't quite up but I'd had the best sleep of my life. "Jillian, I think there's someone outside the window."

We scrambled from the bed, and I grabbed a dress to pull on before going outside. When we rounded the corner, there was a wolf lying right under our bedroom window, sleeping like the dead.

"Hey!" Dean yelled, startling the wolf. "What the hell are you doing here?" He began to step toward the wolf, but in moments, the wolf was now a man, standing in front of us.

And I knew exactly who it was—Shane.

"What's going on?" he asked, rubbing the back of his neck.

"Why are you sleeping underneath our bedroom

window?" Dean asked, voice terse and angry. I'd never heard him so forceful.

"Oh..." Shane looked my cabin up and down before shrugging. "I have no idea. But my wolf kind of does as he pleases. He's a fickle beast. Not sure why he chose to sleep here. Do you have any ideas?"

His question targeted me. No matter how much I tried to deny it, there was something palpable and urgent between us. A tether I didn't know how long I could ignore.

"No? Okay. Well, sorry. See you later."

Shane walked away but Dean was still livid. His jaw was clenched, fists balled at his sides. He had stepped in front of me during the conversation, all protective and fierce.

It was endearing to say the least.

But not necessary.

Shane would never hurt us.

Chapter Seven

Jillian

Dean was grumpy all day after finding Shane outside our window, but even if I'd had an easier time communicating, he wasn't ready to hear the answer. He did ask if I knew him, and I was able to write, *We've met once or twice.*

We were walking toward the compound at this point, both of us with assignments that would take us there that day. The gardens were sprouting like crazy, meaning, I would be weeding on hands and knees, and he was going to be working on the remains of the winter woodpile. With such a good supply, there were still many cords left, but the pack had not left it neat as they made their selections. The bounty made them careless.

We parted midway between the two areas, but we didn't kiss as we usually did. I started to rise on tiptoe, but when he didn't lean in, I jerked back and headed for the carrots. Their leafy tops were growing fast, and since they were popular both with us and with livestock, we didn't need weeds to impede them. And they needed thinning for maximum performance.

Dean called after me, but I ignored him. Partly because I was angry, and partly because I felt guilty. Maybe mostly guilty. He was confused, clearly. I suspected men you barely knew didn't sleep outside your window in human form. Probably nobody did. Of course, I'd never been part of that world, but I did go into town sometimes, and when I was younger, I'd seen some television and movies at the homes of friends.

I dropped to my knees and started down the first row, pulling weeds and pinching off seedlings growing too close together. Unfortunately, the work, unlike my forest gathering, was not engrossing enough to keep my mind on it. Every few seconds, I looked up to see Dean, shirtless in the spring sunshine, tossing logs here and there, the muscles he'd developed since his arrival bulging with his efforts.

My bookish mate had become hot. No shifter looked bad, but all the outdoor work had added definition, and the sweat trickling down his chest, his skin glistening...well, I'd rather look at him than at weeds and dirt.

And it was a good thing I was watching him because just as I had almost convinced myself that I was spending time ogling my own mate when work called, it happened. A female dressed as if she was going to town or something strolled along and stopped a few yards away from the woodpile. I knelt up, waiting for her to move on, but instead, another female joined her, and although I was viewing them from the back, it looked to me as if they were ogling my mate.

I stayed there long enough another of the weeders, Marci, came up beside me and elbowed me. “What are you looking at?”

We weren’t close friends, but I was mad enough to show her. I jerked a finger in the direction of the brazen hussies.

“Ohh, those two. You know your mate has really become the subject of a lot of gossip. Some of the girls are wondering if he’ll take another mate or two. It’s not as common as a female with more than one, of course, but there are always exceptions.” She sighed. “If I didn’t have my Norton already, I might be tempted. Was he always that hot? I thought he was kind of skinny and pale when he got here but, whew...” She shook her head slowly. “He’s not skinny or pale now. I bet he really heats up the sheets.”

Oh hell no. I wasn’t going there. Not going to discuss my sheets and my mate with this middle-aged wolf whose kids were older than him. Luckily, my lack of speech came in handy in cases like this. I shrugged, grimaced, and went back to weeding, letting her make of it what she would.

In time, the two females wandered off, and I settled in, weeding and thinning, thinning and weeding until my back ached and I knelt up again to stretch out the tight muscles. The lengthening sun rays caught my eyes and I blinked, but when I cleared my vision, what I saw had me on my feet and leaping the four-foot fence around the garden on my way to claw the faces off a trio—three!—females who had not only stopped to leer but were closing in on my mate who had gone from piling to chopping logs into usable lengths for those who still used woodstoves all year round.

He straightened and pulled a bandana out of his pocket to wipe the sweat from his brow, but froze. What? He wasn't used to seeing his mate about to yank every hair out of the heads of those mate-chasing whores.

"Jillian," he called. "Stop. Don't."

My hands were inches from a couple of their heads, fingers clawed, and I had been fully ready to wreak havoc upon their persons, but his words slowed me. Didn't quite stop me. I brought my hands down and gave a strong shove to two of them. My mate was not theirs. I'd had nothing in this pack before he showed up. Before we helped each other make a life together, and a trio of randos, a trio who when we were all kids together treated me really badly, this trio was not going to lay a finger on my mate or my life.

F. Them.

"Jillian!" Dean let the axe drop, missing his foot by inches, because of me, because I, who could see another mate, maybe even two, would deny him the same if he chose it. If it was meant to be.

My wolf was howling inside me and I turned and ran, stripping as I did, shifting into my furry self, setting her free to take me home where I could hide my shameful behavior.

They are not his mates, she insisted, leaping over a fallen log. *He is ours, but he is not theirs.*

How do you know? You cannot know that.

I know.

But what if she didn't? What if he was destined to be mated to females who disparaged me? Who had tripped me up and "accidentally" spilled things on me...who had told everyone I was an idiot just because I couldn't talk. Or read. Or do anything nobody had bothered to teach me?

We ran until we couldn't run anymore then walked home, head and tail down, and curled up by the hearth. Dean was there, in bed, but he wasn't asleep.

"Jillian, what happened?"

I was too tired to shift, plus if I could get him to do the same, we could mind speak. After staring at me a long moment, he slipped out of bed, in all his gorgeous nudity, and joined me on the hearth, two wolves, muzzles together, while I told him some things about my childhood.

And those females.

I wanted to talk about Shane, about the possibility that there might me more males for me, but I didn't. As I took comfort in his furry body wrapped around mine, his oath that he'd never want anyone but me, the moment when I could have explained had passed. For now. It would come back around soon.

I just hoped it didn't cost me my mate.

Chapter Eight

Jillian

"Again, Jerad?" Dean growled as we arrived for work the next day to find the beta blocking our way. That morning, as we used the waterfall again as a shower, he'd whispered all the reassuring things I needed to hear.

I was his only mate.

There was no one else and never would be.

He loved me.

"That's not really an attitude you should have about the alpha asking you to meet with him. You best learn your place, newcomer. Now move your asses, the both of you."

Dean grabbed my hand and I groaned inside. I had more meetings with the alpha in the last month than I had in my whole life.

Truth be told, I preferred it the other way.

"Come in," the alpha called out as we knocked on the door. My stomach twisted itself into knots as we walked in. Always happened when I was around him. The alpha didn't call you in to ask about the weather.

He meant business and, as far as I was concerned, Jillian and business added up to nothing good.

"You asked to see us, alpha?"

He harrumphed and leaned back in his chair. "I actually asked for Jillian, but it's fine. You're her mate now so this concerns you as well. I've been thinking about our visitor and I've come to a conclusion. Please, sit down."

We sat in the chairs across from his desk. The alpha scrubbed his hand over his face and blew out a loaded breath.

"With the appearance of this person who is clearly deluded about Jillian and the other strangers who have popped up lately, I want you and Jillian to move into quarters closer to the pack. Having you in the woods, isolated as you are is now dangerous. If something were to happen out there, we would not be able to get to you in time."

I stood so fast, the chair I'd once been sitting in fell over backward and hit the floor. Panic spindled down my spine and infiltrated my veins.

He was the one who put me there. He was the one who basically banished me out there by myself when I was only a child. I had to learn how to take care of myself with only Magda to guide me the best she could.

He made me feel like I was unwanted, unneeded. I was vapor to this pack before, and now he wanted me to move closer for my safety?

I called bullshit. Not even caring for protocol or manners, I reached across the desk and snatched up the first piece of paper I saw, along with a pencil. I scribbled down my anger and jutted it toward the man who was on the line of being my enemy.

He read it and then balled the paper up only to discard it like it meant nothing. "I'm not sure you understand, Jillian. This is an order."

Another piece of paper.

You banished me to my cabin. It's my home now. You've never cared about my safety before. If I need to be protected, I will do it myself just like I've done everything for myself since I was small. If you don't agree, I will simply leave the pack.

It might've been the longest thing I'd ever written in my life.

As he read the note, his eyebrows dipped down, and a grimace formed on his face. Dean leaned forward to read it as well and cringed, taking my hand in his. I could feel his wolf trying to push calm and love into our bond, but I was too shielded to accept it.

No way the alpha was going to do this to me. That cabin, now that Dean was in it, finally felt like home.

"Are you sure about this?" the alpha asked. All of the sudden he wanted my opinion.

I nodded and crossed my arms over my chest. I wouldn't budge, not a fucking inch.

"Dean, you will be on watch then, I suppose. As her mate, you have to keep her protected. She's...it's vital that you do. Do you understand?"

I felt like I was being manhandled. Not that I was the victim of abuse but that the men were handling the situation for the sweet little scared female.

Clearly they didn't know who they were dealing with. Dean should know better.

"Alpha, my mate has done an exemplary job of protecting herself all this time but of course, I would give my life protecting her. We will be fine. I'm sure the man is mistaken."

The older man behind the desk seemed okay with that. Of course he was because Dean said so.

Not caring if they were settled with the decision or not, I stomped out of there.

They'd made me the outcast, and I intended to stay that way.

Chapter Nine

Jillian

The day after the meeting with the alpha, I went to visit with Magda. Shifters aged slowly, but once they reached their final years, things moved quickly. I wasn't sure about her witch half, since I didn't know any others. When I met my friend, she seemed like any other adult in the pack, albeit with more wrinkles and her hair was salt-and-pepper waves at the time. The pepper was gone now, leaving only salt behind, plaited in a single braid that went to her waist.

And her straight posture had been replaced with a bit of a hunch. That was likely because she had to lean on a stick to go anywhere. She'd done so much to help me, and now I wanted to repay the favor.

Since my friend and mentor didn't leave her home anymore, at least no farther than her little yard, I stopped by every day to see what she needed and, I'll admit it, for a hug. Sometimes I was a little jealous that I wasn't part witch like her, but she told me that she'd shared most of what she knew with me anyway, and being a generational witch wasn't all that.

I did suspect she was saying that to make me feel good.

Dean had gone into town with some of the other men to pick up some things for the farm, and I was busy processing some herbs I'd gathered in the forest, so when he kissed me and asked me my plans, I'd waved at the piles of greenery around me and the drying racks I was assembling for the first time this year.

Lately, I hadn't been going anywhere without him, but as I was pounding a combination of herbs for a salve, I heard a piteous cry and the pestle dropped into the mortar. *Magda!* She lived close but not close enough to hear and, knowing only a true crisis could have occurred, I stripped my clothes off as I ran out the door.

Even in wolf form it took far too long to get there. My friend's cries were still with me. She was in pain. I was going to rip the arms and legs off whoever was harming her.

The gate was torn from Magda's fence, and her front door was open wide... Bounding inside, I stopped and looked around. The place was a disaster, all her neat jars and boxes and racks of medicines and spell ingredients tossed around. Not a thing was untouched.

I didn't see a sign of the intruder or intruders who had done this, so I was wavering on what to do next when I heard a moan from a corner. I shifted quickly back to two-legged. I was going to need hands to dig her out of the mess, and my wolf was on full alert for a quick change if anyone returned to cause more harm. In fact, she was snarling, growling, and pacing inside me so that I could barely think.

Please stop. We have to help Magda.

I will shred their flesh from their bones for what they have done.

In fear that my wolf knew more than I did, that Magda was horribly injured, maybe even on the verge of death, I did not worry about finding anything to cover my nakedness before tossing things aside, calling, *Dearest, where are you? Help me find you, please.* I had never communicated with her or anyone in human form, but I had no other way to try.

"Here, by the stove..." Had she heard my thoughts? Or just reacted to my presence. Her weak voice did not reassure me in any way, but it did point me in the right direction. I had to wade through broken furniture and to my horror, the stove was still burning. How easily could this mess catch if only one spark from the open stove door fell to the floor. Dried herbs and grasses were tinder.

I managed to get across the floor and closed the stove before I dug down to find my friend. My every instinct wanted to dig her out first, but if a fire started, we would both be lost. Scanning the debris, I spotted one of her feet, bare and so vulnerable... *Magda, I'm here. Try not to move, I'll get to you.*

She didn't answer that time, and I had to use every bit of self-control to move things methodically aside instead of flinging them madly as I wished to do. If I did not exercise care, I could injure her worse.

Finally, after what felt an eternity, I lifted a shawl to find her smiling up at me. Her eyes in their folds and wrinkles twinkled. Only Magda could look so positive while still half buried under her destroyed belongings. But at least her expression made me think she wasn't in terrible pain. Then she sobered. "I'm glad to see you, I won't lie, but it's not safe for you to be here."

I cleared some baskets and things away and the small table that had pinned her legs and eased her to sit up. I tried to keep her from standing, worried she might hurt herself worse.

"Don't be silly, child. I'm perfectly fine. If you'll assist me to my feet, we can start cleaning up this mess."

Only Magda.

Fortunately, before I could argue, the doorway filled with pack members, led by the alpha with my mate at his side. The alpha brushed past the rest and stomped to my side. "What happened here? We were halfway back from town when Dean went crazy demanding we pull over and save you."

They hadn't shifted to get here faster?

Before I could ask, Dean was there, handing me one of Magda's cloaks. "Here, mate, put this on. We were not far away where the highway borders the lands. Why aren't you home?"

My wolf must have called to his. When we were in wolf form or now? I didn't know if it worked like that, but it didn't really matter.

I shrugged. Since I had no way to write, he'd have to wait for details until we got home.

With so many people there, they had the place set to rights quickly, Magda in her comfortable and blessedly unbroken chair by the fire, protesting all the fuss. The pack members carried off the broken items, and I mourned the loss of so much of her herbs and things. Many would not be replaceable until fall. But I was very happy my friend was not badly injured. The alpha demanded she move to the compound, but she brushed aside his concerns.

"I served the pack under your grandfather, young one. I did it from this cottage where I have lived since I was born and where I will stay until I die. The vagrant who came here seemed to want information about someone named Callista and when I didn't have it, he made a big mess and left."

"Exactly why you shouldn't stay here," he argued, his protests less orders than frustrated requests. "We cannot get here fast enough if you need us, Magda."

"I neglected my wards." Her consternation came through clearly. "I must be getting old, but not so old I cannot put them back in place." She faced Dean and me. "And I will also ward your home. I can do part of it from here and give you instructions for the rest."

She leaned back and sighed. "But I must sleep for a while first."

The alpha tugged his shirt over his head. "You two go. I will remain here until the wards are in place. If that miscreant returns, I will end him." He shifted to wolf and moved outside, waiting until we exited to lie blocking the doorway.

Chapter Ten

Dean had his arm over my shoulder the entire way home. His wolf communed with mine. They were speaking to each other without words, the way animals did, or the way shifters did. It was a simple exchange of emotions and pushes of sensations, but each one got the gist.

His was protective and concerned.

Mine was grateful he came for me, and yet, confident she could handle it on her own.

"I can't believe all of that happened." It seemed like he was muttering to himself more than talking to me. "I mean, one second I was fine, and the next I was demanding the alpha pull over and let me get to you. If he hadn't, it was like my wolf would've gotten out and shattered every window of that vehicle in an effort to get to his mate. Wow, it was just that powerful."

The connection between mates was impenetrable. It was as solid as the ground beneath us. No matter where I went or what we went through, our mating was never negotiable. It gave each of us a sense of comfort and security.

I stopped in my tracks as a variance of new scents touched my nose. Some were sour and tangy, but one in particular, almost layered on the top of the rest was still present.

My wolf knew exactly who it was.

"Jillian, what is it?" Dean stopped along with me, but now that I knew, a stripe of fear spindled down my spine and pulsed through my cells.

Shane might be in trouble. And if he was to me what my wolf thought, then there was no way in hell I was going to not tear down whoever was with him.

Because the scent alone told me they were up to no good.

Fueled by fear, I grabbed the front of Dean's shirt and dragged him along the trail between my cabin and Magda's.

"Jillian, what the..." Dean didn't struggle but questioned me all the way there. When we got to the cabin, all, or most of our things were strewn about. My clothes and Dean's were in separate places and even our kitchen things and pots and pans were tossed about like they were trash instead of my precious possessions.

And Shane's wolf was in the mix of it. He was panting, and his fur had been roughed up by whoever thought it was okay to destroy my home.

"What the fuck is this about?" I hardly ever heard Dean say that word, but the anger was so thick in the air, I almost expected it. This male wolf had clearly protected my home or at least tried to interrupt the destroying of it. "Why is he here again?"

Let's face it. We all knew deep down why Shane was there.

I did.

I'd seen the look in Shane's eyes. He did.

Shift. I said the command in my mind and, in an instant, Shane was on his feet, a bashful look on his face even though I was nothing but grateful to him for at least trying to save our home.

"I...I was protecting your home, Jillian. I was a little too late, as you can see, but I tried."

Dean stepped forward, and I could feel the waves of fury pour off of him and cover the atmosphere around us. "I can protect her. She is mine to protect." He looked around and found a pair of pants tossed to the side, threw it at Shane who put them on. I wasn't sure whose pants they were, just Levi's that could have belonged to either of them, but it didn't matter.

I blew out a breath just knowing in my heart that this could end a few ways, but none of them were good.

"You *were* protecting her. And I was here, trying to stop those miscreants from getting in her house."

A growl came from deep inside Dean. I expected Shane to move or step back, but he did no such thing, Instead, he stood his ground and balled his fists.

"Well, I am her mate, too."

Oh, gods above. Not now. Not like this.

So, I stepped back with the force of the honesty. It took the breath from my lungs no matter how long I'd known deep down that it was true.

"No you're not. We're not one of those harem things. She's my mate, and that's final."

The cheek of this mate of mine. I knew he was hurt and stunned, but telling Shane and me what was final, well, it just wouldn't do.

Shane ticked his gaze to me and so did Dean.

All it took was a look, and the beginnings of tears welled in his eyes. He knew, and he knew that I knew.

"Jillian, tell me the fucking truth." I stood there, paralyzed, while he realized I couldn't exactly answer his request. "Is he your mate, too?"

My lungs failed to do their job. My heart slumped into my stomach, and my knees wobbled.

I nodded. Because he deserved the truth.

"He is your mate, too?" He repeated the question,

and I nodded again. His voice was little more than a whisper, and somehow it slayed me even more than it would if he yelled.

"This is it. I'm in one of those harems. And here I came down on Christie for that, and no...this can't be. I wanted you all to myself. Am I not enough?"

I reached for him, trying to wordlessly assure him that of course he was enough, but fate had a reason for putting Shane in my life. I didn't know what or how, but it was something.

He wrenched his arm away from me, splitting my heart in two.

"I can't handle this. I just...can't."

I watched my mate stomp into the woods as tears rivered down my face.

Wait, who was Christie?

Chapter Eleven

"Now what?" Shane stood there in my upended living room, the cozy home I'd started, and Dean added to the mess. Not as big a mess as the one at Magda's but a lot of breakage nonetheless. "What do we do?"

I shrugged. If he meant about the fact Dean had taken off after Shane declared us mates and I didn't deny it, not much we could do. I'd have to deal with him when he returned. If he referred to the disaster that was my home? I bent and flipped over an upended basket. I was going to clean up. I couldn't even find anything to write on or with at this point. Making communication difficult.

He picked up a bowl and then, after looking around, turned a table right side up and set the bowl on it. "I know you can't talk, but maybe if we clean up enough, we'll find your pad or...have I seen you writing on a whiteboard?"

I nodded, scooping some pretty stones into a little basket before setting them next to the bowl on the table.

"I came to keep watch, and found someone just entering the house, so I followed them in. Before I could get a good look, they shifted, so I followed suit. Thanks for the pants, by the way."

So they were Dean's. Oh well.

"The intruder...I don't even know what they wanted. I didn't get the feeling it was a burglary."

Of course not. What was here to steal? It was a little nicer than it had been, but who would want our new mattress or the frying pan I'd so prized when Dean brought it to me.

"Anyway, we fought, and I got the better of him eventually, as should be obvious, since he left."

We were both picking things up and straightening them as he spoke, and I was really hoping to find any of my writing things soon or even my art supplies. I felt silenced in a way I hadn't in a very long time, and I had a lot to say.

If he was my mate, and I believed he was, we should be able to talk as wolves, but now was not the time to test that. If I didn't get the place straightened, Dean and I wouldn't be able to get any rest.

Dean! He had taken off like a wolf out of a bonfire, singed fur and all. He must be so upset. Although I might be a little surprised he left me here with Shane.

For so long.

I spotted my whiteboard and grabbed it but nothing to write with. I was almost desperate enough to try to use a bit of burned wood from the stove, but feared it might damage the board, so I set it carefully on the windowsill and continued cleaning up.

"Jillian, I never wanted to make any problems for you, but I can't deny what is between us. When I came here, with my brother, we'd been thrown out of our old pack by the alpha. I wasn't looking for a mate, just a place to live and try to fit in."

I spun, arms filled with rumpled clothing, to look at him. He'd been banished? Why? But I didn't know how to ask, or even if it was my place. Of course it was...wasn't it? Did we need to know one another better? But if I was going to upend my hard-won happy life, I thought it might be something I should know. Soon?

"I explained it all to the alpha, of course, I mean we did. It was kind of him to accept us. We've tried hard to show our worth."

Curiosity might eat me alive before I got the information. Maybe I could scrawl the question on the floor with that burned wood.

"I-I don't know what we would have done without

the acceptance we've received here." His voice was laden with emotion, and I recognized this was not a conversation we'd be having in writing. It would have to be mind to mind, and that meant letting it go for the moment. "Is this something we should keep?" He held up a piece of wood that, after some consideration, I recognized as the leg of a chair I'd rescued from a trash pile about a year before.

I shook my head and waved my hand. It hadn't been that good even then, and Dean had wanted me to throw it away anyway.

"Okay." He tossed it out the open door to join the pile of irretrievably broken or damaged items. "I wish we could find something you could write with. It must be hard for you."

My heart beat harder. He got it in a way few did. Not...I wish you could talk. Wish you weren't unable to speak, or my very favorite, what a shame you aren't different than you are. Shane wanted to help me communicate in the way I did. Accepted me as the person I was with my limitations. I didn't know what made his former alpha banish him and his brother, but I decided I would accept him in the same openhearted way. When I stumbled, I'd remember that our alpha wouldn't have taken them in if they had been criminals, harmed anyone. Plus, just a look at his face told me he was not a bad person.

Would someone evil sleep outside my window just to keep me safe even though I hadn't taken him as my mate yet? Sure, fate sent him to me, but the ultimate decision to mate did belong to the shifters themselves.

Would a miscreant have fought off the intruder?

And...would anyone but a kind soul be helping with the cleanup? Of course, Dean would if he were here, and I had no doubt he would on his return. But Shane was new to me. I was just getting to know him. And everything I saw, I liked.

Chapter Twelve

"You've gotten most of it cleaned up." Dean's voice scared me and I jumped. The moon was high in the sky and, if I wasn't mistaken, it was nearing midnight. "Sorry, didn't mean to scare you. I brought back a few rabbits. Didn't know if there was anything left...to eat."

At first, I felt bad for the way Dean had found out that I had more than one mate, but more and more as I cleaned up in sacred silence, I was glad. Now there was no more guilt or wondering what would happen. Dean would either accept it and Shane or he wouldn't.

At least, that was the front I was putting up for myself. I'd already turned over the makeshift island. The cutting board and knife were strewn on the other side of the living room, so I pointed to it.

He took one look at Shane and gave him a dead stare.

"Yeah, I'll get it prepped," Shane said, but he wasn't smiling. Nobody was smiling.

The rest of the night went on like that. My mates, yeah, I was saying that now, weren't speaking to each other. Dean exchanged niceties with me and remained civil, but it was cold in our home, colder than any snow-covered night by myself. My body felt hollow and, at any moment, I might just crumple into myself and fall onto the floor like a wilted piece of paper.

Shane worked in silence, but once in a while our gazes would meet, and he would wink at me.

At least there was a sliver of warmth in here.

"Here, you eat first. We only have one bowl left. Well, one plate too." Dean spoke to me, but it was clipped and cold.

I held up a spoon and handed it over to him. I'd just washed everything in a basin, since most of what we owned had ended up on the floor or outside in the dirt.

Dean waved his hands in the air, but there was no emotion on his face. He was hollow like me. "No, you eat first. It's fine."

Shane hadn't even looked up from the shattered bowl he was picking up.

Mentally and physically exhausted, I stomped over to the whiteboard, picked up a marker, and scribbled down something I wanted to say, erased it because it sounded bitchy, and then did it again. I turned it around and showed Dean.

You eat. Not hungry.

It was the truth. Not only had our home been ransacked, but my skin felt dirty like a blanket of mud was on it. Like I'd been violated. My entire life had been violated and tossed about like my belongings.

That feeling was just skimming the surface of the emotions running through me. Dean walking away stripped me of something, trust maybe. He didn't stick around and face those fears with me. He chose to walk, and it stung more than I was willing to admit.

But he came back, and it gave me hope again.

And Shane was here despite the obvious contempt from Dean.

We could get through this together.

As soon as we dropped the cool-and-collected act and put down our invisible shields.

Didn't seem like that was going to happen anytime soon.

"Eat a little with me, Jillian...mate. My wolf will be all squirmy and demanding until you eat. Um, Shane, there's a plate for you, too."

That had to be a step in the right direction.

He was blaming it on his wolf.

Fine. I would bite.

I sat next to him, and we ate out of the same bowl. It was almost too polite—too icy. We both acted like robots, never touching, never meeting each other's gazes.

Shane finished his plate in record time and washed up his own plate.

Of all days to feel lonely, surrounded by my mates, this was not the day. I needed their comfort and their reassurance.

My wolf wanted a lot more, but she would have to stuff it.

"Jillian, I'm going to sleep outside again, as my wolf. I'll stay by the front door so that..." He looked at Dean who didn't look up at him. "I just don't want to invade your privacy. Good night."

He placed a chaste kiss on my cheek and left. My wolf whined inside me for all that had happened today and for missing her newer mate.

Dean yawned but didn't move from his chair. He just sat there and stared at the fire. No reading. No writing. No teaching Jillian to write.

He just sat there like life had rendered him unable to do anything else.

I knew he was not familiar with shifter culture for the most part, but he had mentioned something about someone else he knew being in a harem.

He must've thought I was a horrible female and

mate.

I wrote a note on the board and set it in his lap.

I'm going to bed.

"Wait, Jillian. I'm coming with you. I just want today to be over."

If I could talk, I would've reamed him out for that comment. He wasn't the only one suffering. He wasn't the only one having a shitty day.

Maybe it was good I couldn't speak.

I changed into my pajamas and crawled into bed at the same time as him. It wasn't that big a bed but as he turned his back to me, he might as well have been on the other side of the continent. I shivered in my cold loneliness and prayed the night would erase this day.

Chapter Thirteen

Dean

"What did I do now?"

Two days had passed since Shane had essentially moved in. Or rather outside. He still slept outside our home as if I couldn't protect my mate, but he ate with us, and whenever he wasn't working on whatever he did for the pack—no, I didn't know or care—he was hanging around the place.

As had become my habit, when things got stressful, I cut more wood. So much more wood. And that's what I was doing when Jerad tracked me down. Not far from the compound, a few trees had fallen in a bad storm early in the winter, and I was making sure it didn't go to waste. It was like a regular day but on steroids.

I'd been turning a tree trunk into kindling with my axe and trying not to think of it as Shane who, according to my mate, was also her mate. And yes, I'd known this was a thing, sort of. I'd had a very odd conversation once back home on the topic and thought it was just the craziest thing ever for a woman to have more than one boyfriend or husband...mate, I now realized.

Some of my friends had been shifters.

And now that I thought about it, Sierra probably was, too.

I knew that now, but had they recognized the wolf deep inside me? If so, they'd never indicated as much. In fact, they'd made a real effort to keep me at arm's length, except for Christie of course.

I missed her. I wanted to talk to her. More than my family even. She'd been my best friend. Could she still be? When people became couples, or more, they tended to fall away from their single friends. Not that Christie had done that to me, exactly. We'd still seen one another at school, had lunch once in a while...

But it wasn't the same. Now that I was part of a couple or a trio? I didn't think it was a menage, since I thought that meant all three were involved with each other. Or were they? I didn't know and didn't want to ask anyone locally because that was hitting too close to home.

The time before I came here felt shrouded in fog, and sometimes it was hard to remember specifics, but I was fairly sure I hadn't been Mr. Supportive on the topic. Maybe if I had been, I'd have learned something and been better prepared for what was going on in my life—in our life—now. So that's where I was when Jerad found me. Lost in thought, confused as hell, and creating what could only be described as toothpicks out of a mighty tree trunk. And the question I was responding with was yet another summons to the alpha's office.

"What did I do now?" Because of course being called to visit the great man felt like nothing more or less than being called to the principal's office. And that never happened because a person did something amazing like, cut enough wood for five packs or fix up the shack my mate was relegated to for no reason she'd ever been able to figure out. "I am in the middle of something here."

"I see that." Jerad was probably more annoyed at having to come find me than anything. The beta never exerted himself if he could avoid it. "But I don't think the alpha will find that a good excuse for not coming as he orders."

"Orders," I grumbled. "Always orders. Is that what being a wolf is about because my wolf seems to disagree."

The rumble deep inside me represented concurred.

But Jerad didn't need to say anything more. I slung my axe in the holster I'd made for the purpose and strode toward the alpha's house. Whatever had displeased him, waiting for me to show up wouldn't help.

And standing outside his office, waiting to be admitted while the rumble of his voice on the phone was not helping my mood, either. Finally, as I was considering leaving, the door jerked open, and he was standing there, glaring at me.

"It took you long enough," he bit out, waving me in. "Don't keep me waiting."

I did not mention who had actually been waiting for whom. I'd been a shifter just about long enough to know better. "Sorry, Alpha." I moved to stand by a guest chair, the protocol dictating that I not sit until invited.

The alpha moved around his desk and sat then barked at me, "Take a seat. I called you here because something alarming happened today. One of the females was taking some food to Magda when she was accosted by a stranger."

I sat but remained straight-backed, wondering why he thought this affected me and afraid I knew. "Accosted? Did he harm her?"

"No, he was looking for your mate. He called her Callista, just like the others, but this one looked dangerous He had a stun gun on his belt and flexible cuffs dangling from his hand. I think this problem is getting bigger."

Oh hell. I agreed.

Chapter Fourteen

There were things that happened when you found your mate. I knew it. Shane knew it. Dean knew it, but things were so tense that I couldn't even think straight.

Plus, Dean hadn't really accepted my new mating. If he did, it would've given me and Shane some time alone.

I desperately wanted some time alone with my new mate.

"Hey, where are you going?" Dean asked me. Shane was puttering around outside, something about making me some flower beds around the cabin. Honestly, I thought he was just making up excuses not to leave me alone—or to wait for a chance for Dean to leave.

Maybe both.

To gather herbs. Some for Magda and some for us. Why? I was sure my scribble revealed my attitude about him helicoptering. He had been like that for days. I knew he had met with the alpha and also that someone was snooping around, apparently after me by mistake, but I wasn't going to live in fear just because of some deranged person.

Also, there was this harem situation.

I was stretched out as far as I could go. Strangers lurking around and attacking my friend—Dean and Shane not speaking and acting like everything was peachy—whatever weirdo was calling me Callista—all of it.

I just needed to breathe.

And yeah, to mate with my second mate. I was going to snap soon.

“I’ll come with you. It’s been a while since we took a walk together.”

Whose fault is that? I was a little pissed at him. He was hovering in a way he hadn’t before. I rolled my eyes.

Maybe it was because of Shane. Maybe it was because of the strangers all around. Who knew? Either way, I needed some time to think—alone.

“Let’s just go and talk like we used to. We used to walk all the time. Maybe we can go to the caverns. You love those.”

And there it was. He wanted things back like it used to be. And in that moment, I did, too. When I could walk out of my cabin without explaining it to anyone.

Not what he meant.

Things change.

Gods, I was being mean to him, my mate. I didn't want to, and it hurt my chest to act like this, but at the same time, he needed to let me go a little. If you hold your mate loosely, there's more room for love to grow. I thought Magda had told me that.

"I can see that. Jillian. There could be someone out there who might hurt you. Whoever hurt Magda might be after you next. They asked about you. They are close. I don't know what I would do if someone hurt you."

Back to my whiteboard where I wrote out something that was even meaner, but I couldn't seem to help myself.

If they come after me, what are you going to do?

I showed him but then erased it and wrote: *Fine.*

Giving up, I threw myself onto the nearest chair and blew out a breath. Dean left shortly afterward, asking me to please stay at home. I had no intention to so instead of agreeing, I simply shrugged.

Shane came into the house right after Dean left. Gods, he was a sight. Not that Dean wasn't, there was just a different attraction there. Dean was my first and would always hold that place in my heart but Shane was something else. He was on the verge of dangerous, or at least, his smile was. He had one dimple on his left cheek and it deepened as he smiled.

The pit of my stomach was sick from having argued with Dean.

"You're going to go out anyway, aren't you, sweetheart?" He smirked, and my insides turned to goo. He called me sweetheart. No one ever had. It was endearing and heartfelt, and I just wanted to run to him and let him mate me right then and there.

I nodded. Going outside my cabin and doing what I did every spring wasn't wrong just because Dean didn't like it.

"Just be careful, okay? Keep those eyes peeled. He's not the only one who would miss you. I haven't even tasted those lips yet."

Oh, gods above. Give me strength.

I couldn't have left in that moment if I wanted to. My knees were jelly, and all I wanted was to kiss him.

We hadn't done that yet and it was killing me.

Mating shouldn't be this hard. It should be easy and lovely and sweet stolen kisses.

Not this tension and denial of what I really wanted just to appease my other mate.

Dean should be supportive of this.

And yet, here we were.

"Come find me if you need me, okay? I'm here for you always." His smile held more worry than his words.

Okay, Shane clearly took notes from some of those books Dean and I read. I walked over and kissed his cheek before picking up my basket. One last look over my shoulder, and I was on my way.

Once I was out with the sun hitting my face and the sweet scent of spring reminding me of my tasks, I was fine. The anger and frustration seemed to seep out of me like dew.

My wolf simultaneously whined for Dean and hungered for Shane. Maybe I wasn't cut out for this harem thing after all.

Chapter Fifteen

I wasn't far from the cabin when I began to wonder how right Dean was about my not being out alone. The alpha had suggested—ordered because no alpha really ever suggested anything—that he accompany me or at least stay close, but I had forced the issue until he'd had to back off. Our relationship was equal with each of us having a say, and if I put my dainty foot down, as I had, I'd left him no choice.

It was a nice day with spring really starting to warm up and dappled sunlight sprinkling through the newly leafed trees, but I couldn't appreciate the weather. Once, my time in the woods gathering things had been the only peace, the only pleasant elements of my life, but now, I had so many more good times. Evenings by the fire with Dean, getting to know Shane, even the women of the pack had started being nicer to me.

Not that they'd been mean.

They had just acted as if I didn't exist.

Now, when I showed up to weed the kitchen gardens or brought in my baskets of things they requested, they smiled at me. Looked at me. Saw me. Since I had no idea why they'd ignored me, I couldn't say why that changed, since they had been kind to me when I was little, at least kind enough to keep me fed and clothed, but I was glad things seemed to be swinging back that way. Less lonely.

I found a cluster of morels near a downed tree and made a mental note to tell Dean where the tree was. Not that every fallen trunk needed to be cut up for firewood or to be refined into boards. With the amount of wood my mate was finding, the alpha had ordered that suitable logs be dragged in and then had ordered a portable sawmill online. When it arrived, Dean had a whole new job, but he didn't find it a chore. I'd caught him more than once inhaling the scent of the freshly sawn boards.

I never picked mushrooms without remembering Magda teaching me how to identify them and all the other types. Morels were a particular favorite of hers and available only briefly at this time of year. She'd get a good amount of whatever I could collect. With this find, I began hunting for more, remembering the places I'd hunted them down other years and soon had a brimming basket of the precious little gems. They looked like fairy houses to me or at least how I'd pictured them.

I wasn't sure if there were fairies or not, and was considering the possibility while walking along, keeping an eye out for more morels—not that I had room in my basket, but I'd never pass them by. They were such a gift from the goddess, and I hoped to find enough for everyone to enjoy a little at least. Suddenly, all thoughts of fairy circles and wings fled my mind.

I heard voices.

At one time, I'd have assumed they were pack, but as crowded as the woods had become lately, I had to assume the worst. Slipping behind a tree, I strained to hear who it might be. With good luck, it would be a few men hunting or taking a stroll, a break from the rigors of this time of year in the fields.

But I'd had all the good luck I was going to, at least for now, because I recognized neither of the tall wolf shifters who clomped into view. I shrank back farther away from the path and gripped my basket tightly.

"I tell you, we can't go back without her this time or she'll tear our heads off." The man closer to me had his fists clenched, his black beard giving his face a menacing appearance.

"So what do you suggest we do?" His companion's

arms hung at his sides, but his shoulders were high, tense, and a snarl marred what might have been a handsome face if it didn't look so mean. He had pale-blue eyes, I noticed. "Run?"

"Don't be ridiculous. She wants this resolved and soon," Black Beard growled. "And her reach is long." They were directly opposite me now and, instead of continuing on as I was praying they would do, they stopped right there. In the worst possible spot.

"Not far enough to keep Callista from being spirited away."

"Far enough to have tracked her here. And we know how she got that information."

Blue Eyes shuddered. "I wasn't there, but you were, I understand?"

"I was." Even his fierce-looking beard couldn't hide the fear twisting his mouth. "And there wasn't much left of him when she and her betas finished. Maybe running is the thing to do. We could sign onto a ship going to the South Pacific or somewhere. If that's still a thing. It was when I was young."

"I don't know. Let's keep that as an option if we fail." Blue Eyes shook his head. "But this shouldn't be so hard. The girl has to be alone sometime. We just have to keep aware."

"And avoid her mate, and the alpha who made it clear we were not welcome on their lands. If he finds us here now, we'll have a different kind of big troubles."

"At least he's not a torturer."

Black Beard's voice dropped low, but I could still hear it. "He may not bite off pieces of us, but he's just as likely to rip off our heads in one blow or have his betas do something worse. We have been named trespassers and... Well, let's not think about it. We need a plan."

They were moving again, heading toward the edge of pack land, and I waited until their voices faded away before scooting out of the brush and running for home.

Was I really this Callista? I wasn't so sure about that, but I was positive I didn't want to go with these thugs to whoever "she" was and probably get bitten up. If her intentions were good, she would not be sending criminals to tear up the place and kidnap me.

Because that was what they were planning, right? Kidnapping me?

I had to talk to my mates.

Chapter Sixteen

"Whoa!" I rounded a corner around a huge oak tree and bumped right into Shane. Broad-chested, mate of mine.

He knocked the breath out of me because I'd run into him, but my lungs refused to work anymore because he was my mate. My handsome, caring, obviously protective, and nurturing mate.

I needed him like that next breath that just wouldn't come out.

Still as a statue, I stood there taking him in. Yeah, I still loved Dean as much as ever, but I also loved Shane. He was my mate after all.

His strawberry-blond hair fell over his eyes a little and, before I knew it, I was brushing it away. He caught my hand in his and brought it down to his lips. My heart thrummed overtime, threatening to jump right out, busting through my ribs. My core tightened and pulsed at once, making me want him to push me against the nearest tree and make love to me right there in the forest.

"I came to check on you," he said. "You've been

gone for hours. I told myself I wasn't going to be clingy but my wolf wouldn't let it rest. But it turns out you're fine, and he was just being silly. Well, you're more than fine, looks like to me."

Oh, gods above, this one was a romantic just like Dean. Different but just as swoony. A rush of heat filled my cheeks and meandered down my neck. He pulled my hand to his lips and pressed a kiss on my palm.

It might as well have been my thighs as much as it revved me up.

"Can I carry that for you?"

I shook my head and shifted, mentally demanding he shift with me so that I could talk to him. I had to tell someone what had just happened.

He stripped—and that made things even worse—before he shifted next to me and, for a minute, we simply reveled in the nearness. Our wolves play bit each other, and he nudged my muzzle with his own, a wolf's kiss if there was such a thing.

Are you okay? Shane asked me through our bond that was strengthening minute by minute.

I saw some men in the woods. They were talking about that Callista person again. They were looking for someone. Said they were waiting for a girl to be in the forest alone—without her mates.

The fur on the back of Shane's neck stood on end. He snarled, revealing some of his white, sharp teeth. *They would die if they touched my mate. They would wish they had never been born.*

While I appreciated the fierceness of his protection, it was unneeded. I could protect myself—always had. *Do you think I'm this Callista person? I mean, who is that?*

You sound just like I imagined you would. Shane lay on his belly and rested his head between his paws. *What do you remember about your birth, mate? I am realizing now that I know very little about you. I want to change that, but your other mate is not happy with the situation.*

I don't remember much. Not a lot at all. I confessed. It was weird to admit that. I had no idea who I was before I came here. I didn't even know if Jillian was my name or if he had given it to me.

And clearly there was a chance my name was Callista.

A snooty name if I'd ever heard one.

We need to fix that. I want both of you to be comfortable with being in our home together. We have to work this out.

He turned his sweet blue eyes to me. *I want that very much, mate. I miss you at night. I yearn to be close to you.*

He shifted back in place, and I followed. Electricity popped and crackled between us as we stood there, facing each other. He was built of pure muscle and as he stood there, they rippled and flexed, letting me know they were there. Not being able to help myself, I reached out and touched his stomach, the valleys and hills there completely still as Shane sucked in a breath through his teeth.

"Mate, you don't know what you do to me. Don't touch me unless you mean it." He whispered the words. He meant them, too. He was fully erect and didn't even mind me looking at it. "I'm not ashamed that I crave my mate."

No, he definitely wasn't ashamed of that at all.

I moved my hand down to touch him there, but he stepped back. "Not today, mate. Not like this. When I take you, and I will, I want nothing but you and me on your mind."

I let my hand fall to my side.

"I changed my mind," he said, chuckling. "Please, touch me. At least let me kiss you."

Oh, gods, I was on fire for this man. He placed his

hands on either side of my face and leaned in, smiling sweetly at me before covering my lips with his. The kiss began as a slow dance, but sooner rather than later, our mouths opened together. He pressed me against the tree, and his proof of lust poked my belly. He kissed like I was the water and he was the fire. Like my mouth and my lips were the only things that could save him.

But as fast as it started, it was over. "I have to stop." He pressed his forehead against mine. We were both heaving breaths, our eyes never looking away from each other. "If I don't, you'll be mated and marked right here against a tree. You deserve better than that. You deserve everything. Gods, you tempt me, Jillian."

He tore himself away as though it pained him and put on his clothes. I did the same and, as I was picking up my basket, a bolt of guilt shot right through my torso. I'd just cheated on Dean—but then again, I hadn't.

Still, I hated this. Dean knew I had another mate, and yet,, I felt some kind of remorse for showing that second mate love.

"Let's go back, Jillian." He took my hand in his and kissed me chastely on the lips. "Yeah, I'm going to need more of that. You're a really good kisser. I knew you would be."

There had to be a look of shock on my face since I was stunned beyond belief.

Dean had never complained, but to hear it out loud...

Now to tell Dean. I had a sinking feeling this was not going to go as well as I wanted it to.

Chapter Seventeen

By the time Shane and I got back to the cabin, Dean was already there, sitting on the rock stoop, his head on his knees.

"Jillian?" he said, looking up as we paused.

Dean's gaze shot right to our intertwined hands. He clenched his jaw and balled his fists. A feeling in the pit of my stomach told me this was not going to go well.

"I can't believe this," he whispered, but I heard him just fine. Shane tried to remove his hold on me, but I didn't let go. Dean had the problem with this, and hiding my mate from him wasn't going to make him get over it any sooner.

"It would be better if you started. You and I are not enemies. We are both here because Jillian is our mate. We should be working together to make her happy. Clearly, that's not happening," Shane spoke, but it all seemed so far away. My heart was beating so hard, I heard it between my ears as though it was in my head instead of my chest.

"No, and it won't happen. I made her happy way

before you. I was here all this time. I am her mate!" Dean rose to stand and pointed his finger at Shane. I looked over at my second mate, expecting him to be fuming but instead, he was cool and calm, muttering something to himself. I would have to remind myself to ask him about that once my mates weren't fighting.

"And I am, too. Put yourself aside and think of her happiness. That's our main goal in life, to make our mates happy. She is our priority, not our anger or our jealousy."

"Fuck you. She's mine." Dean's voice cracked. All of his pointed words and harsh language weren't about being angry. It was about being hurt and having his ego bruised.

"She's ours, Dean."

Dean stomped over to us, and I knew that look in his eyes. Shane let go of my hand and stepped forward, still breathing steady, still calm and collected. He totally needed to give me lessons on that.

"Don't do this, Dean. I don't want to fight, but I won't let you hurt me or her."

That stopped Dean in his tracks. "I would never hurt her." He turned to me. "Jillian, you know I would never hurt you."

Of all the times not to have my whiteboard. I

rushed inside and got it, wrote a note, and then showed it to him.

You are already hurting me.

Dean ran his fingers through his hair a little more violently than necessary while blowing out a breath. "I'm hurting you? How? Tell me."

Tears welled in my eyes. *By not accepting my other mate. It kills me that there is distance between us.*

Dang, I was getting really good at spelling—at least I hoped.

Dean stepped back as though I'd slapped him, but instead of being okay, he turned his rage-filled gaze on Shane.

And before I knew it, he'd reeled back and coldcocked Shane right in the jaw. Shane barely moved under the impact.

Which more than surprised me.

"You need to go cool off—before you hurt yourself or me. Jillian won't be happy about it, either."

Again, without touching Dean, Shane shot him with a dose of the truth. The fact that Dean couldn't accept Shane was killing me, ripping me apart and shredding my heart.

"I just..." Dean looked down at his knuckles, red

and raw from punching Shane. "I guess I have no choice. Mate, this makes you happy? This is what you want?"

I nodded. He knew that already, but clearly Dean was having trouble with acceptance.

"Okay. I give up." He threw his hands in the air and looked down. "I'm going for a walk and then can we all just sit down and talk about this? Some ground rules, maybe? I don't even know."

Shane stepped forward. "Dean, I think that's a good idea. We all need to think a bit about this and regroup. Fate had it in her plan for Jillian to have both of us as mates, certainly we can find a way to move forward for our mate. She deserves all the love we can give her."

Shane was some kind of guru when he wanted to be. Who knew?

"She does." I let out a breath. They were agreeing on something. "She deserves everything. Jillian, can you forgive me? I swear I'll try my best. I swear to you, mate. I love you."

I rushed Dean and hugged him tight. He wrapped his arms around my waist and buried his face in the crook of my neck. "I'm so sorry. I'll make this okay."

I pulled back and kissed him like there was no

tomorrow. He needed a sign that I loved him as much as Shane.

Something we would have to talk about.

"I'm gonna go work some of this energy out. See you later—see you two later?"

Shane nodded. "Yeah, I need to get to work, too. How about we walk together? Get to know each other a little?"

Dean nodded and let go of me. "I guess we should. Let's go."

Chapter Eighteen

All the emotional scenes lately had me exhausted. Shane slept outside again, under the window, and I wanted to insist he come in, but I wasn't sure who would sleep where in our little home, and since Shane and I hadn't officially mated… How on earth did the other females with harems do it? If I'd had any close friends among the women in those relationships, I'd have asked for advice, but even though I was getting a little more warmth from the pack members, I wouldn't say we were close.

My wolf wasn't even what I'd call supportive, since she was sure about who her mates were and had no time for anything else. Mates were mates, and that was that. And I agreed, but agreement wasn't all it took to make a family. Wasn't that what this was all about, after all? My mates and I finding that place between us where we could come together and create a happy home? I needed more information about how to make that work. How to be sure that neither of my mates felt left out or less loved than the other.

I did get Shane to come in for breakfast, but while

the two of them were obviously trying to be good sports, that wasn't how this was supposed to work. I didn't know much, but I knew that they should be comfortable enough to talk over breakfast. To say please pass the brown sugar or offer the other a refill of coffee when pouring their own.

For a girl who'd been living alone in the woods, it seemed overwhelming. I didn't even know how to be part of a family, really. My first memories were with this pack, although I understood I hadn't been born to anyone here. And I'd been passed from one person to the next, raised like a child who didn't belong to any specific mother and father. And that was true. I didn't. But I had to belong to someone, even if maybe they weren't alive anymore. Who? I'd never allowed myself to think about it too much, always focused on making it from day to day.

But the time had come for me to find out where my roots lay. I was a wolf, as were all those in the pack, so maybe I was the product of distant relatives?

Someone's by-blow? Wolf shifters rarely had children with anyone but their mates. It was more than a rule, it was how our minds worked. And our wolves were even more disinterested in a non-mate. But once in a while something did happen, an unexplained attraction or, worse, a rape would result in a child born outside of matings.

Depending on the pack, those young ones might be accepted or might not be. Since nobody paid attention to me, I'd overheard a lot of gossip while working in the garden or other tasks. Nobody mentioned me at all, but maybe there was something I should know.

After all, I didn't appear from thin air!

I sat on the stoop for an hour or more after my mates left for their work. I didn't know much about what Shane did, except it was somehow related to security. But of course, everyone was involved in planting at this time of year. Including me, and with nothing resolved in my mind, I started for the fields on the other side of the compound. We were planting carrots today. A lot of carrots. We sold some baked goods at our farm stand and at the farmer's markets around, and the carrot cakes and muffins were big favorites with the customers. So...we had to grow plenty, but we were going to try out some of the new colors and see how they went. I was kind of excited about that.

Also about the herb garden. We'd had a small one last year, and restaurants had bought every bit we could provide. They were apparently quite profitable. Dill and mint and tarragon and parsley—flat and curly leaf—and so many more.

Usually that would totally occupy my thoughts. But not this year. Everything had changed. Which was why, halfway to the field, I turned off and headed for the alpha's house. If anyone knew where I came from and where my original family might be found, if any of them were left, it would be the alpha.

I passed others on the way to their various tasks, but they weren't any more interested in me than they had ever been before. Still, I studied each fact, watching, wondering...did they know? I mean, if a little girl shows up out of nowhere, wouldn't people wonder why? Had I been left on the previous alpha's doorstep in a basket like some movie, or had he taken me on at someone's request. If so, who?

If I was going to start a family with my mates, and since Dean and I were doing it every night, and Shane likely to enter the mix soon, a baby seemed like a definite possibility.

I felt like I needed to know about my birth family. It might not be a pretty tale, but I thought I was mature enough to hear it. If I was really Callista, what did that mean? Odd that I'd been here all these years with nobody showing up to collect me and return me whence I came and now...now the forest was filled with people who wanted "Callista."

By the time I arrived at the alpha's house, I'd built up quite a head of steam. I was going to march right into his office and demand the information I was due. Everyone had the right to know who they came from. I reached for the front door just as Jerad was coming out, laden with bags of seeds.

"Jillian, aren't you supposed to be planting carrots?" he huffed. "I am sure I saw you on the schedule."

I nodded.

"Good." He piled his bags in my arms. "These are the tricolor seeds for the experimental area. Take them with you."

I pointed frantically at the alpha's house, gripping the heavy sacks as they threatened to slide from my arms. I did have my whiteboard in my satchel, but I'd have to drop the seed bags to get to it, and I wasn't sure I'd be able to pick them up again.

"The alpha is out there already. You can talk to him there." Okay, he understood me.

Because this was a topic to address surrounded by others. For sure. Without further hope of communication, I turned and headed for the field, knees wobbling under the weight of the carrot seeds. I'd have to learn my origin story another day.

Chapter Nineteen

I had a notebook in my back pocket and patted it as I approached the alpha. Since he was surrounded by other pack members like he was a celebrity instead of our leader. He answered questions while patting his rounded belly and laughed when he was supposed to, but to me, an outsider for the most part, it all came off insincere and stiff, like he was simply putting on a show.

I supposed that's what celebrities did.

While I waited for my turn, I looked out over the fields. From this vantage point, I could see my mates in each of their occupations. Shane was bent over a row of bok choy of all things, picking out weeds and, every once in a while, swiping sweat from his brow with the back of his hand. He didn't wear gloves. When he scooted over, I saw the pools of sweat that stained his shirt and the dirt that marked his knees. He was a hard worker but would smile and make small talk if another pack member spoke to him.

I gasped as he looked up just as I was thinking about him—stalking him. A smile tugged at one side of his mouth, and he gave me a curt nod. My cheeks heated up like we were in the woods again, him naked, and me pressed against that oak.

"Jillian, you were waiting for me?" I jumped a good four inches in the air and, if I had a voice, I would've screamed.

I nodded and pulled out my pen and raggedy notebook from my back pocket. He was a busy man, and the last thing I wanted to do was to get more negative points for wasting his time.

Would you mind if we moved so that the others can't hear?

"Of course." He began to walk away from the fields of vegetables and legumes and toward a small copse of trees. "There. We should be out of earshot. What's on your mind? I can't remember a time when you actually requested a moment with me." He chuckled. "The others can't seem to stay away and you...well, go on. I'm sure you have better things to do."

I furrowed my brow at his attitude. It was so off from who he regularly was, but then again, I supposed he did have to put on airs for the others.

I saw those men again in the woods, calling me Callista.

He stepped forward. "Did they hurt you? Did they

see you?"

No. I'm fine. They were passing through but I don't think it's the last time.

"Maybe you should consider staying close to your mates when you roam, Jillian." I felt my eyes widen, and he chuckled a little. "Yes, I'm well aware that there are mates, plural. And honestly, it's a good thing. The pack is happy for you. I know they keep their distance, but it's for a reason."

Why are they after this person? Callista?

Hells bells, I didn't even know if I was spelling the name right.

"I really don't know what they think they are accomplishing, Jillian. I think they are just shooting in the dark. Maybe one bullet will hit something. Until we know and can catch them, please stay close to someone. I know it's in your nature to be a lone wolf, and most of that is my doing, but for the near future, stay with Shane or Dean. Okay? Look, I've got some things to take care of. Let me know if you see them again."

I stomped as he walked away. My questions were avoided in the most diplomatic way possible and yet, I had stood there and taken it.

This pack stuff was frustrating as hell.

Since I had a bit of a lull in my work, I decided to cross the fields and talk to Dean. I could hear the slicing of the axe through the air and the crack of it as it penetrated the wood, splitting it into pieces, so I followed the sounds to my mate.

I stopped a good distance away and waited for him to see me instead of taking the chance of frightening him. Last thing either of us wanted was an axe incident.

"Jillian?" I didn't have to wait long.

I waved and smiled at him. Gods, he had changed since I first found him in the woods. His chest had filled out despite our meager food, well, it wasn't so meager now that he was getting rations from the pack. His arms, once scrawny and skinny more than lean, were now rippled muscle and bulging biceps. He had his shirt off and, despite the still cool temperatures, I was getting flushed just looking at him.

Gods, he was mine.

How did I get so lucky?

"You keep looking at me like that and no more work is going to get done today." He had come over and bent down to whisper in my ear, his specialty.

My notebook and pen were still in my hand so I wrote him an answer. *Like what?*

He chuckled and kissed the side of my neck. His lips were cool against the heat of my skin, and it made me shudder. “You know like what, sweetheart. Like you want me to take you right here on this stump. Like you want to eat me all up.”

Maybe I do.

That did it. One moment I was standing there with him in the woods, and the next I was over his shoulder like a sack of freshly plucked potatoes. He patted my butt while he carried me toward the cabin but stopped once we were in a more private area.

“I can’t wait until we get back to the cabin. I have to have you now. There’s been too much tension between us. I feel like I’m going to snap.”

Chapter Twenty

Dean

Jillian and I were alone for the first time in a while. Even though Shane was sleeping outside rather than in the cabin, his presence loomed large. And, as a result, our nightly lovemaking had all but ended. Not that my mate rejected my advances but more that I didn't make any.

Shameful as it was, in a culture I was told found females with multiple mates to be not only acceptable but in many cases preferable, I found this downright distressing. I mean, growing up in a human world, I'd only been around two-person relationships. At least that I'd been aware of. Likely there were plenty of alternative relationships but in our small town, if there were, those involved kept it to themselves.

Not in the pack! I'd seen females kissing each of their mates as they left for work and greeting them on their return. Major PDA. But it wasn't the sex that made me envious. Not that they had sex around others of course, but some of the kissing and hugging and things left no doubt what they planned to do when they were alone.

As I was now, with my mate.

Her skin was soft and carried the scent of spring green plants and a bit of woodsmoke. The scent of home, but if I couldn't truly wrap my head around the fact she had a second mate, I would lose her. I hadn't known I was a shifter long but long enough to understand the fact I couldn't deny her what was hers by right, Shane. A gift of the goddess I'd only begun to know.

Searching around, I found a mossy spot near a stream and laid her down. Her eyes were half closed, her arms outstretched toward me, and everything worrisome fell away. We fumbled with our clothing, laughing at the awkwardness of buttons and zippers catching in our hurry.

The sunlight filtered through the tree canopy, casting shadows on her skin as it was bared to my eyes. We'd made love outside once or twice, of course, but it had been cold for most of our time together. Today, the air held warmth promising that not too far off, summer would arrive. We'd have plenty of cool days between now and then, of course, but today was perfect for what I had in mind.

Jillian tipped her face into the sun, eyes closed

and a smile tipping her lips, but then she sat up, blinking at me. She reached for her bag, dragged out the whiteboard. *We're both supposed to be working. What will the alpha say?*

I pressed her back into the soft green bedding. "I don't care."

She struggled to rise again, but my palm flattened between her breasts. *He will be mad. Will send someone to find us.*

"Jillian, we passed him on the way out of the field." I held her gaze. "He winked when I tossed you over my shoulder. I think he knows what spring does to people. It's a time of hard work, I'm learning, but also a time for love."

Despite herself, she smiled. *Yes, and I love you very much.*

"I love you, too. Does that mean you're going to put down your marker and let me do this?" I trailed my lips over her jawline to her ear and nipped. "And this?" Her throat, her collarbone, then I rested my cheek on her warm, silken breast. Toying with her nipple between my thumb and forefinger, I blew a soft breath over the peak. I skated my other hand down her belly to cup her mound, one finger dipping between her labia to barely touch her clit.

Jillian's breath hitched and her hips rocked, but I didn't let her have her way. My hands went no farther. I'd learned my mate liked to be kept waiting just a little sometimes. She might deny it, but when I played with her for a while, she came like the explosion of fireworks.

Her eyes pleaded, requiring no words. Sometimes, I didn't speak, either. But I did have one more thing to say.

I took her nipple between my teeth and rubbed the flat of my tongue over it, grinning at the shudder that rippled over her. "More of this? Or shall we go back to planting and chopping?"

Her hand closed around my cock so firmly, I had no doubts of her decision. Just kissed her with everything in my heart and soul, showing her instead of talking. I'd talked myself blue, and she'd nearly worn out her board with trying to express her feelings, but for this? I kissed her everywhere, appreciating the brighter light. Her skin had an opalescence, sort of, not really sparkling, maybe a glow? Or maybe it was just what being in love did to a man.

When she was writing and gasping, and her strokes on my cock were seconds from driving me over the edge, I peeled her hand from me and rolled onto my back, bringing her with me. She straddled me, rising on her knees and then sinking by millimeters, tight, hot, and mind-blowing. I brought my arms up and linked our fingers, as she rose and lowered herself taking more with each descent until I was buried deep into her body. She leaned forward to kiss me, and I released her hands and gripped her hips, helping her to move, helping her to engulf me, helping us both to ride the tide toward completion.

I wanted this to take a long time, but after just a few nights of not having her, it might as well have been a century. I was so primed, I wasn't going to last long, so I freed one hand and plunged it between her legs, rubbing her clit in fast, tight circles until, even muffled against my lips, her cry startled a flock of small black birds in the tree above us into flight. Her inner muscles clenched, milking me of every drop of cum and eliciting a howl that no kiss could suppress.

She stayed there, lying on top of me, until my cock shrank back and fell free of her, and then she stayed there some more. After a long time, the breeze kicked up, and it became too cool to be naked. The sunlight was slanting at an angle that told me afternoon was well underway, and while the alpha might be understanding, he also had jobs to get done.

Jillian must have had the same thought because she sat up, climbed off me, and reached for her clothes. I did the same. I would have loved to shift and run, but while the alpha was patient, he had limits, and our work waited.

As I worked at the sawmill that afternoon, preparing boards for an order placed, my mind was all over the place. I just couldn't relax and accept Shane into our little house. It was very little more than a single large room, and Jillian was the first girl I'd ever felt completely comfortable with.

Sure, Christie was a good friend, and Wendi, but they were just that. Friends. Kind, caring friends with multiple mates, both of them. And when we'd been together, I hadn't yet known I was a shifter or that the only real way to find happiness in love was with mates. So I'd been kind of annoying, hitting on so many girls, just hoping to have someone special in my life. I yearned for things I didn't even know existed. My crush on Sierra might have been just because of what she was, although I knew now that it hadn't been anything like the feeling of a mate.

If I was going to move forward to the next steps in

my new life, I needed to get some advice from friends, and that meant friends who would understand.

Next time I was in town, I would call Christie and see if we could get together. With her mates. I needed advice if I wasn't going to mess up the best thing that ever happened to me.

Chapter Twenty-One

Jillian

Dean was working overtime, but because it was a Saturday, I was hankering for something to do. I'd plucked just about all of the morels and stocked up on other needful herbs from the forest for both me and Magda and honestly, just didn't want to do anymore.

Shane was puttering around in my little herb garden outside, but since he worked on it every day, there wasn't much to be done. He was trying hard to be part of things without stepping on Dean's toes, but I wasn't sure how long he could keep that up. He was a wolf, too, and I was his mate. Patience was a very human emotion; wolves were not especially gifted with it.

I picked up my whiteboard and headed outside. Shane's head popped up as soon as I stepped foot out the door. He smiled at me, and my heart fluttered.

Want to take a walk with me? It's a pretty day.

I'd wanted to write beautiful, but I couldn't convince myself that I knew exactly how to spell it.

"I'd love to take a walk with you, mate. Where to?"

He stood up and dusted off his hands on the outside of his thighs. He was a simple guy and I'd noticed even his wardrobe was minimalist. From what I could gather, he had about five pairs of jeans, all the same with the exception of rips in different places, and T-shirts in neutral colors that boasted mountains or sunsets. One of them had some kind of surfing contest thing on the back. He didn't strike me as the surfer type, but these were the things I wanted to get to the bottom of.

I shrugged. Yeah, I had an idea about where we should go, but I really just wanted to move around, enjoy the beautiful spring day. Enjoy the sunshine.

Soak up the stolen time with my mate.

"Doesn't matter. I've been craving some time with you. Dean isn't coming home right away?"

I shook my head and made a pantomime of him chopping wood. He wasn't exactly working with the axe anymore, but Shane would get the point.

"Okay. Let's go, then."

As soon as I sidled up next to him, he took my hand. His warm palms were calloused. Mine were as well, and our callouses fit together like a puzzle made of a history of hard work. My whiteboard was tucked under my arm just in case I might need it, but honestly, I hoped he would do most of the talking.

"This place is gorgeous. When we first came here, I took a walk on the east side of the pack lands. I was so caught up in just walking around and admiring everything that I ended up lost and in trouble for not working. Jerad nearly bit my head off. Still, when I have a free moment, I try to go there and enjoy it. Well, that was, until you. Then I found myself lost in these woods. My wolf knew what he wanted, but I was aimless until I surrendered to him. He was right."

I smiled, feeling my cheeks burn.

This place was beautiful. Every tree had a character of its own. Every leaf a different color in accordance with the level of sunshine it got. I knew every root, the ones that tripped me and the ones who felt like friends.

When I was a girl, I spoke to them in my mind and, while neither of us could speak, I hoped they understood me. They were the only ones who tried.

He stopped talking and, immediately, I missed his voice. I pulled us to a stop and wrote on my board.

What pack did you come from? How old are you? Parents? Family? Friends?

He chuckled as I scribbled down about a hundred questions. "Okay, okay. You want the full story. Good thing we have time."

While we walked, he did tell me everything. He had come from a pack where the new alpha had gotten power hungry since his father had passed. He was a slave driver for the most part, and while Shane didn't shy away from work, he drew the line when the alpha began to force girls to join his harem. They weren't his true mates—he was just greedy.

"It became too much. Girls were plucked from the fields daily like they were ripe tomatoes or something. We never saw them again. He kept them all in a big room, or that was the rumor, like one of those movies where the king has dozens of women at his disposal. Someone said one of them found their true mate and when the alpha heard about it, he had that male killed. Creek and I came this way, trying to find a pack. Others fled north. This place just called to me and Creek. Now I know why."

He jostled our joined hands and winked at me.

We spent the entire day together. I showed him the caverns with their gorgeous crystals, and we shared sweet kisses along the way before heading back. My time with him had gone too fast.

We stopped at the river where Dean and I showered. I dipped my toe into the water and was happy to find it lukewarm. The sun had done wonders.

"Wanna go for a swim?" he asked, already taking off his shirt.

Hell yes, I did. In seconds, we were naked and I jumped into the water first. When I emerged from the depths, Shane was in front of me. Droplets of water clung to his long lashes and made his skin shimmer.

"Come here, mate. Gods, I've wanted to hold you for so long."

He wrapped his arms around my waist, hefting me flush with his body. I locked my ankles behind his back and circled his neck with my arms. Our lips were mere inches from each other. I nearly drowned in his blue eyes, noticing the specks of gold I'd never seen before. He had a small scar above his left eyebrow, and I moved my arm to run the pad of my thumb along it.

"I fell and hit my head on a brick when I was little. It was summer. Bled like a motherfucker. My mom came unglued. A few months later, she passed on. They said it was cancer, but my dad was convinced it was some kind of witch's spell. I didn't know. I just missed my mom. She made the best peach cobbler."

Note to self: *make this gorgeous man some peach cobbler*. As soon as the peaches were ripe. Or...maybe I could use some of those we'd canned last summer. If any were left. Because I didn't want to wait months.

I reached up and ran my fingers through his wet hair. His hardness bobbed between us, and I wanted this—wanted this mating more than anything. I leaned forward and kissed him, tightening my legs around his waist, pulling closer and closer, not wanting anything between us, not even a drop of river water.

"I would mate you right now, Jillian. I want to so badly."

My eyebrows bounced, asking him the question my mouth couldn't.

"Not until you get things squared away with Dean. It's not fair to him or to me or to you. I know he says it's okay, but you only have to look at his hunched shoulders to know it's not. But there are other things we can do. Ways to please my mate."

He lifted me and gently laid me down on the bank of the river. My legs dangled into the water, and he stood there, all of me bared to him. After taking my mouth again, he paid attention to each of my breasts, loving them like they never had been.

"Spread your legs for me, mate. I need to taste you."

I swallowed against the rock in my throat and hesitated. Dean and I had had sex, and we'd explored some things, but this was new.

"Jillian, sweetheart, you are gorgeous. Please, let me do this for you. I can sense your need. Please, mate. Give me what I want. Let me give you what you crave."

His whispers killed me. I lay back, resting my elbows on the ground behind me, and opened my knees. He rubbed his hand over his mouth like a hungry wolf about to get his dinner.

Shane peppered kisses onto my thighs, slowly and torturously moving upward as he did. My legs opened wider of their own accord, and I threw my head back when his lips touched my clit. "There you go, Jillian. Let go. Take what I'm giving you."

The sun beat down on our naked bodies while he lapped at me. Again and again, he drove me to the brink, only to stop right when I was at the edge.

"You want to come, mate? Is that what you want?"

I looked at him. Gods, the sight of him alone was enough to make me come right then and there. Nodding, I sat up slightly and fisted his hair, pulling him right to the place I needed him most.

I gasped as he slid one finger and then two into me, still flicking his tongue against my clit then taking long, slow drags. He flattened his tongue and moved it in a slow, steady rhythm while his fingers pumped in and out of me.

Tingling started at my core and bloomed out, ignoring all my cells while goose bumps broke out along my wet skin.

Then it happened. I shattered against his mouth, grinding my pelvis against his fingers as though it was his cock instead. My entire body pulsed, and I saw stars for a few seconds before blinking against the sun.

He moved back and pulled me back into the water.

"Gods, you are gorgeous when you come. I can't wait to take you."

Dean needed to come to terms with me and Shane and this harem before I exploded. Yes, Shane's mouth against me was a dream, but I needed more.

I needed all of my new mate.

Chapter Twenty-Two

For the first time, my presence was requested at a pack business meeting. I was way too excited to be attending a function everyone complained about all the time. The women I worked with in the gardens claimed they took up valuable time when they could be doing something more important. The betas were always rushing around making notes, when a meeting approached, speaking in low voices and trying to seem very important when everyone knew they were just putting together some information for the alpha. And the young males were even worse. But I had been too young to attend when I moved into the woods and then, other than as a pair of able hands and a strong back, they pretty well all forgot about me.

But both of my mates were attending, and so I guess it would have seemed weird, deliberate even, to exclude me. Sometimes I wondered what I did to be treated as a second-class citizen. Nobody invited me for coffee or to birthday parties or anything at all. Were they trying to pretend I didn't exist?

Either way, better days were coming. I heated

water and got out a bar of soap Magda made and gifted me. Scented with lavender and golden from an oil infusion of calendula from her garden, it was my favorite and I used it sparingly to make it last. But today was special! I washed my hair with the bar as well, rinsing it twice before lathering my skin. When every inch of me, including under my fingernails, was clean and smelled like flowers, I got out and wrapped a towel around myself.

My hair had gotten quite long, and I considered trimming it but then decided now was not the time to take a chance on a bad chop job. Instead, after combing out every tangle, I plaited it in a complex braid of no fewer than eleven strands. By the time I finished, my arms were aching, but I thought it was worth it. I tied the bottom off with a bit of ribbon for fancy.

I had better clothes than I used to but still a limited supply. Dean had brought me a very pretty shirt from town on his last trip. It was maroon cotton, so soft, and laced at the neck. I paired with my long denim skirt and Chucks, a gift from Shane, then spun in front of the mirror, wondering if it was quirky adorable or just completely off-base. But just as I was thinking of changing into jeans and a tee, wolf whistles startled me so much, I bumped my hip into the table.

"We're sorry." Dean ran up and steadied me, but Shane, although he'd been part of the whistling, stayed by the door. As always. "You look nice."

"You do," agreed my other mate. "And we'd better get going. I don't know about this pack, but my old alpha had people whipped for arriving late."

I gaped at him. Was that a thing? Were we running late? I couldn't imagine our alpha having anyone whipped for anything short of maybe murder, but what did I know? I'd been out here in the woods missing out on the good and, apparently the bad, of pack life.

"Really?" Dean was asking the question for me. "For arriving late at a meeting? That seems extreme."

"It probably is, but things were not exactly fun and games there. Note that Creek and I left. A narcissistic alpha makes for a very unstable pack."

"I feel very lucky I ended up here." Dean changed his shirt and ran a comb through his hair. Shane's hair was damp; his shirt was also clean. He must have changed wherever he lived. Actually, he pretty much lived in our yard, so...he must keep his things somewhere else. I felt a pang at the thought that my mate was not able to be comfortable in our own home.

That would have to change.

Dean grabbed a hoodie. "Even if nobody is getting beaten, we'd better start out. It's disrespectful to be late, and I don't want to make that kind of an impression. It's only my second meeting."

I'd nearly forgotten Dean had been to one meeting without me. It had been not too long after he came here, and he hadn't said much about it, leading me to believe there were secrets involved, but he just grumbled about long-winded speeches and people who would argue about whether the day was partly sunny or partly cloudy.

But I didn't let that bother me. Delighted to be included for once, and to be going with both my mates who seemed to be displaying their best manners, I flounced down the path, enjoying the swish of my skirt around my ankles. It was a gorgeous, windy afternoon with the sun playing peek-a-boo with the clouds scooting across the sky.

While we weren't late, we weren't the first to arrive, either, and we ended up having to sit right in the front row. As we passed all the others, I could feel their stares on us and didn't know what to make of it. Was my appearing at a meeting that shocking?

It seemed the front was not a popular spot, but

three seats together were available only there. Dean sat to my right, Shane to my left, and we were no sooner settled in than the alpha appeared at the front with Jerad and Ruston flanking him.

"I looked for that guy for months," Dean muttered, jerking his chin at Ruston. "He was supposed to assign me work, and finally I had to get Jerad to do it. And you know how hard it is to get Jerad to do anything."

"I heard Ruston was away for a while, and not with permission," Shane told him. "Rumor has it he nearly lost his status."

But there was no more time to talk about betas because the alpha called us to order. He brought up a few items of business that were indeed boring, unless maybe you knew more about what was behind them. How many acres of what compared to last year, who was in charge of the farm stand for the summer, and a new quartermaster. I hadn't been sleeping well, worrying about my mates being able to make peace, whether Magda should still be living alone, and whether I was Callista, and my eyelids were fluttering closed when I suddenly felt the alpha's stare join those behind me. Everyone, I knew without turning around, was looking at me.

Suddenly it didn't seem so awesome to be included.

I waited for him to say something that related to me, but my name never came up. Not specifically. Instead, he said, "We've been having some encroachments lately, and it's time to set up a patrol to end this. We do not tolerate any of our pack members being menaced and the damage done to Magda's place was completely unacceptable."

Now the meeting was interesting.

Chapter Twenty-Three

Dean

My palms grew sweaty. I knew what I had to do, but my heart and my wolf rebelled against it with everything they had. Still, if I wanted to give Jillian all of me, it had to be done.

"Can I talk to you?" I asked, stalking over to the garden where Shane put in overtime. It was his gift to Jillian, that much I could tell. When someone is working on something for their mate, others could just see it. It was in the way he spent extra time, fishing out the weeds one by one.

When she looked at it, he practically beamed like I did when I brought home firewood or a freshly killed rabbit.

There were two reasons for what I was about to do.

One: I really thought these two deserved a chance at being alone. After all, we lived in a one-room cabin. But even if we didn't, even if we lived in a mansion, it would still feel too small. That was my mindset talking. There was a barrier, a fence topped with barbed wire, inside me that I just couldn't hurdle.

No matter how hard I tried to get over myself.

"Sure. What's on your mind?" Shane stood and dusted off his hands on his work pants. I'd noticed he tended to finish his other assignments early.

"I need you to give this to Jillian but not until tonight. Gives me a few hours to get away."

His face blanched. I held the envelope with Jillian's name on it in front of me, and when he didn't take the damned thing, I shook it a little.

"Don't do this, Dean. It's going to break her heart. She loves you. Anyone can see that."

I shrugged one shoulder and fought my anger. "Doesn't matter. She'll have you."

I had a mate and new amazing abilities. Bitterness shouldn't be inside me, and yet it bubbled and gurgled from a fountain I just couldn't cork, no matter how hard I tried.

In my mind, it was okay, Jillian and Shane. Just because she loved him didn't mean she loved me less. If I tried, I could work out the details and logistics until it made sense to me. But then my heart got in the way. It was jealous and bucked against any thought of it.

Jillian's harem and my part in it was a heart issue.

"It's not the same and you know that. She'll never feel complete, her or her animal, unless both of us are around. We both have roles to play in her life. It's going to crush her if you leave."

I blew out a breath as the spring wind whipped me in the face, trying to slap some sense into me.

"But I'm not worth anything to her like this. I'm bitter and jealous and angry. I have to learn to let go so I can learn to come back and hold on tighter than I ever have before."

He took the letter from my hand and stuffed it into his back pocket. I knew I was putting him in a predicament by making him the messenger, but leaving it on her pillow seemed cold. What I was about to do was cold enough without adding to it.

Shane kicked at a pebble in the path between lettuce rows. "You still love her, then?"

I scoffed. "Of course I love her. I'm doing this so I can get my shit straight and love her better. Love her like she deserves. Love her despite and because of the fact that I'm not her only mate. I can't do this until I get my head screwed on straight."

He stepped forward with steely rage in his eyes. My chest tightened, thinking this was it, he was going to lay me out right there and beat the shit out of me.

"When you come back, you make sure you're steady with this, okay? She will be able to handle this because she's the strongest female, or male for that matter, that I've ever met, but you don't get to break her heart over and over again while you find your balls. This better be a one-time thing, or else I'll end you. I'm saying that as her mate, someone who is supposed to defend her and protect her. You get me?"

His voice was terse and strong, and I believed every word he said. Actually, my respect for the man grew a hundredfold in that moment. Jillian would be in good hands while I was gone, that much I knew.

Me? Yeah, I still wasn't sure if I had the nads to leave.

"If you're going to do this, you'd better do it fast. Once her wolf alerts her something is up with you, she's going to go berserk." I paused and hefted my backpack onto my shoulder. "I'll take care of her. I swear it."

I shifted and took off at a run with my backpack in my teeth. My wolf wasn't pleased, and that was the understatement of the century.

Leaving Jillian would be the hardest thing I'd ever done.

Chapter Twenty-Four

Shane

No matter what I'd said to her other mate, as I watched Jillian read the letter from Dean, tears trickling down her cheeks, I wanted to go find him and beat him until his eyes swelled closed and his lips looked like one of those Hollywood celebrities with lip-filler gone wild. Nobody should hurt my mate this way.

I'd struggled all afternoon not to open the envelope and read the letter, not to just throw it away and tell her what he'd said in my own words. That he loved her and was going away just to make himself right for her. That was the gist, wasn't it? But somehow, I couldn't do it. I stuffed the envelope in my pocket and tried to go back to gardening but finally gave up and sat on the stoop, leaning my back against the door. I had no idea what would happen—or precisely what was in the letter burning a hole in my pants.

Despite my anxiety, I'd been up since well before dawn and working hard, and as the afternoon sun warmed my cheeks, my eyes closed. I woke to the crunch of a shoe on the gravel pathway to the door and jumped up.

Jillian was carrying her basket, piled with some sort of herbs. I knew about gardening for flowers and vegetables, but the art of herbs was not in wheelhouse. She cocked her head to the side, one brow raised in question.

"I have a letter for you…from Dean." I fumbled in my pocket and yanked out the crumpled envelope. "Here." I thrust it at her. "It's from Dean. He said to give this to you."

She let the basket fall, but I swooped to catch it before all her hard work spilled onto the ground. Tearing at the flap, she moved into the house but then came out again. I knew why. Unless someone lit a lamp, which we rarely did during the day, it was a bit dark to read in the cabin. I wasn't in there much but enough to know that.

Jillian sat on the bench Dean made for her under the flowering cherry tree near the fence. I could have sat there, but my worries had made it more of a stoop sitting time. She pulled out a single sheet of paper and bent close, lips moving as she read the words.

Most people learn to read and write very young, but Jillian hadn't had any schooling at all to speak of, and considering Dean had only begun teaching her a few months before, she was doing very well. A pang of guilt jerked my stomach muscles. He was so much better for her than I was. Why didn't I just say I'd leave and let them be? But I knew why. My not being around wouldn't make me any less her mate. Not at all.

After a while, Jillian looked up from the page, her eyes shimmering with tears.

"C-can I read it?" I wasn't sure I had any right to ask, but she held it out to me.

I sank down beside her on the bench and read the words that made my mate cry.

Dear Jillian,

First, I want you to know I'm leaving for you. That didn't come out right, but I don't have another piece of paper to start fresh, so...let me try to explain. I've been doing my level best to be a good mate to you and to understand that you need us both, that we are both your mates, me and, and him.

But I didn't even know I was a shifter until last winter, and the only reason I learned about mates was by falling in love with you. I'm aware they are two different thing, but kind of the same, I think.

It is going to take me a little time to come to

terms, and I don't think I can do that right here while you are forging a bond with him. So I called my friend Christie, in the town I came from, and we had a long talk. She has three mates, and her friend Wendi has four. I think it's four. Anyway, I'm going to go visit them and see how they live. How they make it work between them. Of course, they don't live in a small cabin, so I imagine privacy is less of a problem, but I don't even really know that.

Heck, for all I know, they all sleep in a giant bed.

I really hope that's not the case. Christi said her relationships with each one of the guys is separate, yet together, they are kind of a family. Makes my head spin, but I want to know. I want to learn.

I want to be the best mate for you possible. I'm pretty sure I'll be back because I'd die without you. Of that I am sure. But if I cannot get it together, I have no idea what to do. Let's be positive. I'm going to visit friends who will help me, kind of like therapy...or research? Also, I can pick up any of my belongings that might still be in my old place, if my roommates haven't stolen or tossed them. And withdraw from school. Lots of loose ends when you run away and turn into a wolf unexpectedly.

Ha ha.

Anyway, the most important part of what I want to say is this. While I'm figuring things out, I want you and Shane to move forward, to do whatever is right between you for mates. Call it a honeymoon just for the two of you and I'll try not to think about it.

We'll get past this because I love you and you are worth anything. It's just hard now, and I think this is for the best.

Please don't try to contact me. The address where I can be reached is on the bottom of this page, also Christi's cell number, just in case of emergency.

I love you, sweetheart, and this is harder than anything I've ever done, but like I said, you're worth it.

Yours,

Dean

Chapter Twenty-Five

Jillian

I watched Shane read the letter from Dean. I hoped it was the right thing to do, letting him see it, but having more than one mate made them family to each other also. And he'd apparently known more or less what was going on. The pity in his eyes when he handed the envelope to me said it all.

"Do you want to go inside?" He folded the letter carefully and slid it back in the envelope before handing it to me and standing up. "It's getting a little cool."

I hadn't noticed, but now that he mentioned it, the breeze was raising goose bumps on my arms. I nodded.

"Do you want me to come in with you?" He tried to make it sound casual, but I heard the yearning. He'd waited so patiently, and tonight...tonight was our mating night. It felt weird to be doing it just because Dean left, but we'd held out for this long because he was here. His discomfort at the feelings growing between us, the pain in his expression if Shane and I held hands or laughed together over something...it was hard to take.

I stood, too, and offered him the best smile I had. I didn't want him to feel bad, or that I'd only take him when there was no other choice. I'd craved him as well, especially since the time in the water when we…when he…when he showed me a whole new level of pleasure. I wanted to return the favor. But mostly, I wanted to cement the bond. I wanted to mark and be marked. My wolf had been pacing for weeks inside me, and the moment Shane wrapped an arm around my waist and led me into the cabin, she lay down and curled up. Easy in the moment. Wolves were funny, or at least mine was, about sex. I didn't know if that part of me had another life, or sex, but I knew when I was with Dean, she'd never seemed to pay much attention when we were making love.

He closed the door behind him and turned to face me in the dimness. "Jillian, you don't have to do this, you know? We don't have to mate tonight just because Dean gave us a permission slip." Bitterness was in his tone but not his eyes. "It's up to you."

Without the ability to speak, I used body language a lot to make myself understood, especially before I became adept at writing. In this moment, I used it to let my mate know how much I wanted him. I didn't need a permission slip from one mate to love another and as I flung my arms around Shane's neck and wrapped my legs around his waist, I wasn't acting on anything the note said. Mates did not have to ask one another for an okay to be together, although they did tend to be considerate of one another. And when Shane's lips descended on mine in a searing kiss that burned away every bit of hesitation left in my soul, there was nobody in the room but him and me.

He carried me to the bed and unbuttoned the top buttons on my blouse before grunting in frustration and yanking the two sides wide, sending buttons flying. His kisses trailed down my jaw to my collarbone where he sucked gently before reaching around to unfasten the hooks on my demi bra. I expected him to damage that, too, but he managed to free it without shredding it. As I stood topless, he straightened and grinned.

"I'd like to do this slowly, to take all night just to reveal your lovely skin a fraction of an inch at a time, but I am afraid that if I do, I'll embarrass myself."

If I'd had my whiteboard, I might have asked what he meant, but it lay in my basket outside, buried in herbs that I was fairly sure wouldn't survive all night piled up like that. And normally, I'd have been bundling them to hang from one of the racks and dry. But this time, they'd have to wait because I wasn't going outside for the herbs or the whiteboard or anything else. I was not leaving my mate here with his cock straining against the flap of his pants and a drop of moisture showing through.

No...instead, I dropped to my knees and reached for the button then lowered the zipper to learn that my mate was not wearing undershorts. How convenient. His cock was shorter than Dean's but thicker, and in its own way every bit as impressive. It jutted out at me in invitation, and I closed my fist about it and brought it to my lips, anxious to learn his taste, to show him that I wanted to give him pleasure, too, before we marked one another.

His groan when I closed my lips about the deep-red head made me smile, which in turn made him shudder. I licked tentatively, rewarded when his knees wobbled and he planted his hands on my shoulders, shifting me so he could sit down and stationing me between his thighs.

I sucked on his cock, taking in a little more at a time then retreating, listening to his breaths become pants. He liked it as much as I had when he'd had his mouth on me, and that was quite a lot. I sped up, my head bobbing up and down, licking and sucking and scraping the edge of my teeth as well.

All too soon, he tucked his hands under my arms and lifted me to my feet. I tried to go back for more, but he moaned. "No, I don't want to spill in your mouth, at least not now. It would delay the mating."

Laying me on the bed, he carefully removed the rest of my clothing with shaking hands before stripping himself much faster and with more damage than even to my blouse before climbing on the bed and urging my thighs apart. Kneeling between them, he watched me with such awe, such love, and such lust, I turned away, but he reached out and cupped my jaw, bringing me back to face him.

"I've loved you since the first time I saw you, and I will love you forevermore. I never dreamed I'd find someone like you." He guided his cock to my opening and paused then plunged deep inside and let out a sigh. "You're everything to me, mate."

Our lovemaking was fast after that, and I'd gotten so wound up sucking on him, I came on his third thrust, again on his twentieth, and then again when he poured his cum into me. I didn't count the thrusts, but I was pretty sure I was right.

And when he came, he bent and sank his teeth

into my neck on the opposite side from my other mark. I bit him as well, lapping the wound closed afterward so it would stay. He was mine, and I fell asleep in this mate's arms for the first time, in love and happy.

I woke in his arms as the bright spring sun poured through the windowpanes. They were small so it didn't reach every corner, but at this time of day, we had more light than any other. My mate's arms were tight around me, and when he stirred, I laid a string of kisses on his chest. It was wonderful to be with the one I loved, but the other was not far from my thoughts. The reprieve of our mating night was over, and while I felt pretty sure we'd repeat our lovemaking many times, my wolf was starting to pace again. She wanted both her mates, all of us together, and she'd never let me rest until we were.

But for now, Shane was propped on his elbow, studying my breasts, as if there'd be a test on the subject, and I hoped we'd stay in bed all day. Dean had his own demons to face, and he wouldn't be able to be part of this family until he bested them. He was strong and kind and loving, and I was almost sure he would return to us.

If not...I had the address where to find him, and I

wouldn't be writing a letter. I'd be showing up at the door to fetch my mate.

"Are you sore, mate?" Shane's voice broke into my thoughts. "We had a strenuous night."

In answer, I held my arms out to him, ready to feel him inside me again and again. I'd never have enough of my mate. Of either of my mates. We'd make it work. We had to.

Thank you for reading *Rejected by Blood.* Next in Series is *Rejected by Birth*!

An Excerpt from Rejected by Birth

Chapter One

I never thought Dean would stay gone so long.

At least I knew where he was. With the Midnight Alder pack, trying to get his head on straight. But when he left, I expected a week, two at most. He left in spring, and we were now in high summer. Crops were growing tall, the baby farm animals in the barns getting bigger every day. And I hadn't even received so much as a letter.

Had he decided he couldn't cope with sharing me with Shane? Although I dug deep inside, I couldn't find a spot of guilt. Mates were bestowed by the goddess, the gods...the fates...different shifters described it in various ways but we all accepted that receiving this connection was to be prized. And enjoyed.

All shifters except, apparently, Dean. Not that I could blame him, entirely. The poor guy had grown up woefully ignorant of his heritage. His parents were human. He either had a shifter ancestor whose genetics had chosen him as a vessel for their latent characteristics, or perhaps there had been a mix-up in the hospital. Or maybe he was adopted and his parents had never admitted as much. For some odd reason, humans sometimes hid such a thing as if it were shameful instead of joyous for parents to bring a child into their home. Either because they couldn't have their own, or maybe because the child was in need. To me, it was something kind and glorious and should never be hidden.

"Jillian, are you coming in?" Shane stood in the doorway, tall and handsome, kind and responsible, great in bed, and everything a girl could want in a mate. Was it greedy to cast one last look toward the woods before going inside?

I lifted the basket I'd set on the ground beside me. I needed to get these hung up to dry before I started dinner.

Shane met me halfway to the house and slung an arm around my shoulders. "Better idea. How about I start dinner while you take care of your herbs?" He dropped a kiss on my head and started indoors.

I blinked at him. He'd tried a few times so I knew for a fact he could burn water. Our woodstove was difficult for the uninitiated, and I gave him slack for that. I handed him my basket and pulled out my whiteboard and marker *Are you too hungry to wait a little? I can do the herbs after dinner.*

He held the door for me, and I stepped inside then paused, waiting for my eyes to adjust to the dimness. Our home was far nicer than it had been before my mates came into my life. It still had bundles of herbs hanging from the rafters everywhere lending that dusty, sweet, spicy scent I loved, but beneath them the furnishings were comfortable and neat. White muslin curtains fluttered in any passing breeze. The bed was piled with soft, comfortable quilts, and we had a nice woodstove for cooking as well as, of course, the hearth.

Waving to Shane to leave my basket by the door, I cut up the rabbit my mate had brought home and thoughtful skinned and left ready for me to work with. Braised rabbit, cabbage, and some boiled potatoes would make a fine meal for us both. As well as the berried I'd picked early that morning from the brambles deep in the forest.

"Are you sure you don't want me to do that, Jillian?" I was chopping onions, carrots, and celery for the braise when Shane came up behind me and wrapped his arms around my waist. "I think I'm improving."

I didn't answer that, having seen zero signs of improvement. And it wouldn't take me long to get everything ready. This was one case where not being able to speak was helpful because anything I said would likely hurt his feelings. Shane wanted to help so much; he was kindness incarnate.

Name one other wolf shifter who would have held back waiting for the female's first mate to get over his hesitation. Not that Dean actually did get over it. He tried. He said he did. But I prayed every morning and night to the Lady that the Midnight Alder pack would help him adjust to shifter life in a way we at Crystal Canyon had not been able to.

His family lived not far away, as well, and I wondered if he would find time to visit with them. Or if he was ready for that

Honestly I didn't care what else he did as long as he found peace within himself and came back to me. His absence left a large hole in my heart.

An Excerpt from *Rejected by Fate*: Mated in Silence Book 1

Chapter One

Jillian

Silence was golden, especially in the caves that surrounded our pack. The familiar drip-drops of water as it melted and splashed into the puddles below was like a symphony to me. The sun barely grazed the edges of the cave, making the crystals that peeked out from the rock glimmer and gleam as though they were communicating with me, welcoming me to their sacred place.

I'd come to the woods to gather some mushrooms the autumn coolness had provided, along with some herbs for Magda, but no matter how determined I was to stay on task, these caverns always drew me in like a moth to a spider's web. One step inside, and I was caught.

Putting my basket on the nearest rock, I whirled around, taking in the place while the sun hit my legs, warming me. I had only one tattered coat and I'd foolishly decided the evening wasn't quite cold enough for the covering.

I should've known better.

Barely pulling myself away from the magnetism of the cavern, I picked up my basket and turned, determined to make it back to my tiny cabin before nightfall. Stew was bubbling in a pot over my fire, and my bed was already calling my name.

Basket in hand, I whirled and waved to the cave before getting back on the path that would take me home. I'd worn a trail into the dirt from all my time coming to this place, so getting back was nothing.

My footsteps were the only sound until a scratching and whining from my left made me freeze in place.

Someone was out here with me. I didn't scare easily, and most probably it was one of the pack cubs who had lost his way, but I wasn't allowed around them unless I was working.

They would have to find their own way home.

A bush next to me moved, and I jumped back, holding my hand to my chest. Two breaths later, a wolf emerged from the thorny bush. He was yelping for help and, as I crouched to put my basket down and get a better look at him, I realized it wasn't any wolf I recognized.

This one was rogue.

Extending my hand, I waved my fingers, trying to coax him toward me, but the male wolf was shaking in fear. And my own wolf was preening inside me, pacing with anticipation. Somehow, she knew this wolf even though I had no recognition.

I patted the ground next to me as I sat down, hoping the more submissive posture would let him know that I wasn't a threat. On bloody paws, he crept closer but only a few steps.

To my right, the sun dipped low in the sky. Night

was falling. This wolf was in no shape to stay outside alone, and the autumn winds would nip at him through the darkness, letting him get no sleep. I had to do something, even though taking someone into my domain screamed against ever fiber I was made of.

Still, the wolf called to me in ways other than his whining.

He needed me. And my wolf knew that somehow he was important.

Maybe he would be more willing if I shifted. Showed him I was the same as him.

I shrugged off my sweater and ripped jeans and shifted right there as he watched. He backed up a few steps before coming near again as my wolf took over my body. The male wolf sniffed me and gave a tiny yelp.

Come on. Follow me. We don't have all day. In fact, we have little day left at all.

I barked once, a command for him to pay attention, and he heeded. I took my basket handle in my teeth, along with my clothes, and began a slow walk toward my cabin. I hoped he would follow, but if he didn't, well, I wasn't going to stay in the cold all night wishing he would.

Using my sharper wolf vision, I looked back

several times to see him now following me, slowly, but still, making the trek. When we arrived at my cabin, I transformed back to my human self, taking my finds in with me. I pushed the door open wide, beckoning him to come in. This was either a young wolf or...maybe a wolf who hadn't shifted before. The fear poured off him like warm molasses. He scented of pine and molasses, actually. Like tang and sweetness all mixed together.

Huh. Hadn't come across that scent before.

Hitting the door with my hand, I signaled for him to hurry up, or at least, that's what I hoped it conveyed.

As I shut the door, closing us both inside my warm cabin with the crackling fire, the consequences of my actions blanketed over me. I would get in some real trouble for having a rogue inside my home.

Still, I couldn't just let him be cold and frightened outside. That kind of callous behavior just wasn't in me.

I knew how it felt to be cold and alone. It wasn't a feeling I would wish on anyone else.

The wolf was shivering in place and I sighed. This shifter was clearly having trouble making the transition back to human.

With a sigh, I shifted back to wolf right in front of him and then back to human. I did this several times while he watched in awe.

After the fourth or fifth time, he finally made it happen.

"Thank you. You helped me. Thank you."

I beelined for my room and pulled out a pair of baggy sweatpants to cover him. I wasn't shy about nakedness, none of us shifters were, but this was a male and I was alone at home. No male had ever come into my cabin, much less a naked one.

"Oh, thanks. I shredded my clothes when I...I'm Dean, by the way."

He stuck out his hand. I swallowed against the rock in my throat, tamping down the desire to take his hand in mine, to touch him and be touched. It had been so long since I'd been touched.

Instead, I lifted my hand and waved, like a complete loon.

"Not much for words, huh?"

I breathed out and shrugged one shoulder.

It wasn't just him. I didn't speak to anyone. It wasn't like I didn't want to—I simply couldn't.

I'd never spoken, as far as I could remember.

Trying desperately to change the subject, I pointed

at my stew still over the fire. My cabin was only one bedroom and tiny at that. In a few steps, I'd gotten him a hand-carved bowl and spoon and was dishing him out warm venison stew that steamed and filled the space with its decadent scent. My cabin was made of logs from the forest around me, and I survived on what I could find from the land. Being a wolf who hunted certainly helped, but my belongings were few, and my life was simple. I kind of liked it that way.

"Oh, thank you. This smells really good. Aren't you going to eat?"

I shrugged and nodded. Yeah, I was going to eat. Right after I got some clothes on. In my haste, I'd remembered him but forgotten I was stark naked.

Not talking and naked. What a sight I must be to him.

Almost to my bedroom, I stopped in my tracks when I heard him take a first bite and groan at the taste. He liked it. It warmed him and fed him.

Tomorrow, I would make him leave before I got into trouble with the alpha. Tomorrow, he would be gone. And, for some reason, that made my heart ache.

Also by Mazzy J. March: *Veiled Wings*, Book 1 of the Sciathain Academy

I grew up human...

But I am fae. A little fact my parents failed to mention the entire time I was growing up. Then when it was time to apply to college, when all my friends were taking the SAT, I was informed that would not be necessary. I was a legacy to the Sciathian Academy, a private college so exclusive, I would find it in none of the brochures in my high school counselor's office. No need to fill out an application or take the SAT. They apparently had their own tests... No financial aid forms because the families who sent their children there had funded the school with a legacy a long time ago. No need to do anything but show up and settle into my dorm.

Pretty sweet. Also a little concerning

Especially when the private jet lands at an isolated airfield and I am ushered into a long, black car along with three other girls who all seem to have known one another since kindergarten and who are chattering away in another language. Gaelic, I think. And since I'd just left behind everyone and everything I knew, this did not bode well for the future. If everyone spoke this language, how would I even attend classes? Or pass a test?

As if Fae Academy wasn't hard enough, there are three guys that all want to date me.

Wait, do fairies date? I think they have soul mates or something. Heck, I don't even know what my powers are yet. I was never in the spotlight in high school, so why in the world am I the shining light here?

Just when I decided to buckle down and study to be the best fairy I can, the whole world breaks open. For some reason the headmaster thinks I am the one who can intervene. I can't even move a pebble or conjure up a rain cloud and they want me to save us?

Dream on.

I'm not the Fae for the job.

About Mazzy J. March

Mazzy J. March is a fan of all things paranormal—shifters, vampires, witches...dragons and all the many creatures that inhabit the world beyond the ordinary. She has been plotting her Academy and RH stories for a long time and is thrilled to finally have them releasing and ever grateful to the readers who are offering such support and helping her dreams come true.

Connect with Mazzy!

Subscribe to Mazzy's newsletter for news of upcoming releases, free stories, contests, and surprises!
Follow Mazzy on Bookbub:
Follow Mazzy on Amazon
Friend Mazzy on Facebook

Printed in Great Britain
by Amazon

40637036R00101